All My Suspects

LOUISE SHAFFER

BERKLEY PRIME CRIME, NEW YORK

ALL MY SUSPECTS

A Berkley Prime Crime Book / published by arrangement with the author

PRINTING HISTORY
G. P. Putnam's Sons edition published 1994
Berkley Prime Crime edition / July 1995

ISBN: 0-425-14770-3

Berkley Prime Crime Books are published
by The Berkley Publishing Group,
200 Madison Avenue, New York, NY 10016.
The name BERKLEY PRIME CRIME and the BERKLEY PRIME CRIME
design are trademarks belonging to Berkley Publishing Corporation.

PRINTED IN THE UNITED STATES OF AMERICA

10 9 8 7 6 5 4 3 2 1

For Mom, who taught me to
have dreams

And Roger, who shoves me until they
are reality

My thanks to:

Detective Sergeant Al Sheppard, NYPD Major Case Squad, Dr. Stephen Connally, Commander Willima H. Alle, Sherry Aaron, and Trev Fuller, who all acted as problem solvers as well as advisers;

Diana, who is always there, and Ellen, who cannot be thanked enough;

Chris and Colin, who have filled in the one big gap so beautifully.

And a special thanks of the how-did-I-get-so-lucky? variety to:

Eric Simonoff, my agent, who read a manuscript on the basis of a phone call and then pulled off a miracle;

And Stacy Creamer, my editor, whose enthusiasm, smarts, and sensitivity were matched by her incredible patience with a first-timer.

All My Suspects

Chapter One

Looking back I realize I should have expected something. Not what happened, of course, but something. Because things were going too well. I'm not a pessimist exactly, but when my life goes too well I usually start checking the sky for lightning bolts—or at the least kamikaze pigeons. A shrink I once saw told me I suffer from early narcissistic trauma, but then, she bit her fingernails.

It was a beautiful October morning, the kind that makes New York City feel the way the inside of an apple tastes, and I was as close to perky as I get. I managed to snag a taxi that the former Princeton linebacker who usually dominates the morning cab competition on my corner was going for, and I positively chirped as I gave the cabbie the address of the ABN Broadcast Center on the Upper West Side.

I'd had a lot of reservations about taking the job with ABN; even as I was signing my contract there was a voice at the back of my mind telling me that I was going to be sorry if I went back to work as executive producer of the soap opera *Bright Tomorrow*.

I took the job because I was scared; I hadn't found steady work since I'd walked off *Bright Tomorrow* five years earlier and I was starting to have the anxiety dream I get where my mother sits

on the edge of my empty bathtub while I'm stark
naked and tells me I'll never work again because
I quit the Catholic church when I was fifteen after
Father Ruggerio told me that no woman would
ever be the equal of even the dumbest man. Then
in my dream Mama begins flying around the bathroom singing the "Italian Street Song." Vocally
she's a dead ringer for Anna Maria Alberghetti.
The significance of this nightmare will be lost on
you unless you know something of my history as
the younger half of The Singing DaVito Sisters in
the early sixties.

So my reasons for going back to ABN weren't
altogether healthy, especially when you consider
the way I felt about my direct superior, our un-
lovable and unloved Vice President in charge of
Daytime, Gregg Whithall.

But things were working out. Or so I thought.
Of course Gregg and I were fighting again, but
that was to be expected. Loathing Gregg Whithall
was part of my daily routine. The feeling started
every morning right before I brushed my teeth. Far
more important was the way I was getting the
show back on track. The new storylines were
strong, our new stud was knocking them dead in
the focus groups as long as we kept his shirt off,
and after extensive negotiations with the hairdress-
ers' union I'd finally won the right to fire the
woman who was making all my ingenues look like
Farrah Fawcett before she discovered serious act-

ing. I was even handling the personal problem of working with a head writer who had been the only lover I ever wanted to marry until he eloped with a twenty-two-year-old girl who gazed at him the way Nancy Reagan used to gaze at Ronnie and who had legs that started under her armpits. The legs I could have handled, but there is no way I ever could gaze at anyone that way. Furthermore, it never occurred to me that anyone might want me to. Or that I might want someone who did.

Nothing has ever hurt the way that did. Nothing.

But I was coping. Granted, my dentist had made me get one of those plastic mouth guards to wear at night so I wouldn't grind my teeth in my sleep, but what the hell: it was better than dreaming about Mama and Anna Maria Alberghetti. And the bottom line was, I was happy. Totally, mindlessly happy. Because I was working again. And nothing can really get to me when I'm working. I used to think.

My cab pulled up in front of the glitzy barn which houses all ABN television production for the East Coast. I paid off my driver, marched up to our fancy entrance, slipped my ID card into the security lock, and entered our spiffy lobby. There I battled my way through the small forest of trees which someone had decided was appropriate decor for a building in the heart of Manhattan, finally reaching the security desk which is known fondly as Checkpoint Charlie. It is called that for the huge guard named Charlie who mans it.

Charlie's been a fixture at the Broadcast Center since it was built in the early eighties. Somewhere in his desk there's a book listing everyone who works in the building but I've never seen him use it. It is a point of honor with Charlie that he can put a name to a face for all of the five-hundred-some-odd souls who regularly work within the Center. Anyone he doesn't recognize he puts through a security check worthy of the CIA.

That morning he was three deep in extras who were working as wedding guests on one of the two other soaps that shoot in the building, so he waved me past without making me sign in. I proceeded to the locked brass door at the back of the lobby which leads to our studio on the first two floors. The locked elevator on the side wall leads to the five floors above us and keeps them secure. All this security coupled with the foliage gives our lobby a weird ambience—sort of penal colony cum *Better Homes and Gardens*. I try not to dwell on it.

I slipped my ID card into the slot, the heavy door swung open, and I inhaled a deep happy breath; I was back in my domain.

I love the feel of a t.v. studio in the early morning. There are maybe a hundred people racing around trying to do two days' work in four hours. At some point every morning somebody will throw a tantrum and announce that there is no fucking way they will ever be ready and they can't fucking work like this, but somehow it all gets done. And throughout it all everybody's beating a path to the coffee cart, smoking, gossiping, and bitching. A t.v. studio is like home, only better, because you don't have to deal with blood relatives. God, I missed the old place for those five years.

Every morning I do a quick tour of the place. I tell myself it's a part of my hands-on leadership but the truth is I just get off on all the excitement. Of course, on that particular day I was going to have enough excitement to last me several months, but I was blissfully unaware of that then.

I began my rounds as I always do by checking out the soundstage. This is the large space where the show is actually shot. Our soundstage is 11,342 square feet and covers most of our first floor. It can accommodate four to six full sets, and in the early morning it resembles the footage in one of those news reports which begins, "Nature struck a cruel blow last night . . ."

Various crew members waved and shouted greetings over the din as I made my way through the debris. In the center of the room Vinnie Santucci, the crew chief, and Mitch Glazer, the lighting designer, were having a creative discussion.

"Move your fucking ladder so we can finish putting up the fucking back flats," Vinnie was bellowing.

"We can't even hear ourselves over the fucking walkie-talkie, you're making so much fucking noise," Mitch was screaming.

It was business as usual. Made me feel warm all over.

I moved over to the prop table where Tommy Props was going over his lists with his assistant, Nate Bernstein. Tommy has worked *Bright Tomorrow* since the first day it went on the air in the sixties; at that time there were two Thomases on the crew, and Tommy Props was nicknamed to distinguish him from the other one. It's been so long since we called him anything else, I doubt if even he remembers his last name. He turned at my approach, his sad old leprechaun's face creasing into a sweet smile.

"Good morning, Miss DaVito," he said. Tommy refuses to call me Angie no matter how many times I ask him to. He doesn't hold with the boss getting too familiar.

"How're you doing, Tommy?" I asked, but I already knew the answer; his hands were shaky and he looked kind of gray.

Damn, I thought. Tommy fights an ongoing battle with the bottle, a fight he periodically loses. Obviously last night he'd lost.

"I'm just fine, Miss DaVito," he lied.

"Terrific," I lied right back and got the hell away. In spite of our years of friendship I've never had the guts to ask him what sets him off or if I could help. I think he knows I've protected him every time Gregg has insisted he be fired, but we simply do not talk about it. The way I see it, it's none of Gregg's damn business. Tommy never misses work and on the rare occasions when he's too sick to function, Nate—God bless him—covers. I mean it's my show, right?

I left the soundstage and made a fast trip across the hall to the wardrobe room where Marc Landry, our own personal Bob Mackie, reigned with the aid of two assistants who were the Mutt and Jeff of the costume world. Boo Dudley is a lanky Texan, blond and over seven feet tall in his boots, who can whip up a formal gown at his sewing machine in four hours. Magda, according to the scuttlebutt, originally came from Hungary. She's short, as dark as Boo is fair, and as round as he is long. Not a sparkling conversationalist, she tended to limit her comments to words of one syllable, but she was a whiz at the last-minute repairs and alterations that are a constant requirement for the costume department of any soap. Boo and Marc go back forever; Magda had been with them for about six months. As I came in she was sewing silk backing in the lace cups of a teddy.

"Make sure we cover the nipples," Marc instructed. "I've already had Program Practices up my ass once this week."

Magda nodded without looking up from her swift tiny stitches, and Marc turned his attention to me. He ran his fingers through his beautifully permed locks and flashed me the smile he uses when he wants me to up his budget.

"Angela, my angel, you know I never listen to gossip," he began. I bit my tongue. In his lifetime Marc Landry has single-handedly elevated gossiping to an Olympic event.

"Of course you don't, Marc," I agreed.

"However, I couldn't help overhearing . . . well,

the rumor is we're bringing back the Claire Win-gate character. . . ."

I felt myself stiffen. "Where did you hear that?" I asked.

"Angelcakes, it's all over the industry. The grapevine has it that we'll be bringing her back younger, like thirty-five, which I must say I think is positively inspired. I mean, Jesse Southland would have been somewhere in her late forties by now, wouldn't she?"

"Jesse would have been fifty-three," I said grimly.

"Jesus! Well, thank God we're fixing that. Anyway, when you're ready to cast I know a to-die-for actress, we did Williamstown together and she . . ."

"Forget it, Marc," I snapped.

"I promised her . . ."

"It is not going to happen," I said.

"But Gregg has been putting out feelers . . ."

"Before I allow Gregg Whithall to bring back Claire Wingate as a goddamn teenybopper, blood will be shed." It was a statement which, given what happened later, had to be a heavy contender in the Famous Last Words Sweepstakes.

Marc was about to start pumping me for dirt when Magda broke in with what was for her a verbal torrent. "I finish," she said in her heavy accent. "Now I go get dirty laundry."

I ducked out of wardrobe while Marc was in-specting Magda's handiwork. I was pissed about the Claire Wingate thing—that it was common knowledge—but I shook it off. I told myself that this time I'd deal with Gregg. He didn't want me to quit again, so that gave me leverage. Of course the catch was, I didn't want to quit. Not ever again. Which gave Gregg leverage. So we were going to go to the mat. Again.

I headed toward the makeup room. I really like to make myself visible there. Sylvia Morris, who is a genius with the greasepaint, had a bad problem with coke a few years back. When she was at her worst she did a little dealing to pick up spare change. She's now supposed to be clean as a whistle and has recently discovered Jesus. Nevertheless, some of the actors who sit in her chair are very young and I always believe in being safe rather than sorry. I poked my head into the room, but she was seated next to her open kit ostentatiously reading her Bible, so I figured all was well and made a quick exit without disturbing her.

Out in the hall again I grabbed a bagel off the cart and headed upstairs. My office is on the second of the two floors allotted to our show. To get to it I have to pass by the rehearsal hall. As usual I gave the closed door a wistful glance as I trotted by.

There's nothing I love more than sitting in on a rehearsal. For me, that's where the magic happens, when the actors make the words on the page breathe. But I've learned over the years that I'm an intrusion in the early morning. Actors need to hang loose and kid around when they're rehearsing a soap opera. If the producer shows up, they start behaving like members of the Moscow Art Theater reworking The Lower Depths. And the final show at the end of the day has all the excitement of televised golf.

Directly across the hall from my office are the two meager cells occupied by my line producers, Babs Deering and Eric Sondergras. They function as my seconds in command, overseeing the details of the daily shooting, and standing in for me if I must be out of the studio. Most line producers spend their off hours praying for an executive producer somewhere to die or retire. I know I did when I was one.

"You're late," my assistant, Nan Robinson, announced as I walked into my office.

"Like any good general, I have been boosting the morale of my troops," I said with dignity.

"Sooner you than me," she said. Nan has no sympathy for the creative process. A wife and mother of three, she probably has the most normal life of anyone connected with Bright Tomorrow. I think she'd be happier working for a large accounting firm somewhere, or maybe an insurance company, but she stays on because she knows that I could never make it without her. Which gives her license to treat me as her fourth, not quite bright, child.

She clucked at me a couple of times and shoved a sheaf of memos under my nose. "Read 'em and weep," she said.

"I just got here," I moaned. "Have mercy."

Nan sighed. "Suit yourself," she said. "But allow me to mention that at least half of these little honeys are from Gregg's secretary reminding you that you are lunching with the great man today."

I'd made a plan to have lunch with Gregg several weeks ago before he started the Claire Wingate bullshit.

"Oh God, Gregg," I said.

"Only in his own mind," said Nan.

"I don't want to have lunch with Gregg Whithall."

"Who does? But that's why you get the big bucks."

"Nan, give me a break, I need some sympathy here. You know what he's going to do to me, don't you?"

"He's going to try to ram Claire Wingate down your throat along with your pasta primavera."

"I'd like to strangle him with my bare hands," I said.

The words were barely out of my mouth when we heard the scream.

The sound, high and terrified, seemed to be coming from the star dressing room which was used by our leading man, Steve Robbe. Nan and I looked at each other for one startled second and then started to run. The star dressing room is the only dressing room on the second floor and we made it there in well under a minute. Actually I think Nan got there first, but I pushed her out of the way so I could see Magda who was by now having hysterics and babbling in Hungarian. Because stretched out on Steve's makeup table, neatly surrounded by Steve's toiletries and the custom-made leather makeup case Steve's lover gave him last Christmas, was Gregg Whithall—who was stark naked except for a gold lamé rose, which had been attached to his penis with two black velvet bows. The wire stem had been used quite cleverly as a splint. Even I could tell that Gregg was very dead.

Chapter
Two

As it turned out, Gregg hadn't been strangled. He'd been shot. At close range with a twenty-five-caliber pistol. At least that was what we were told later. As I stood in the doorway of the dressing room with Nan and the sobbing Magda, all I knew was that Gregg was too still and a color I'd never seen before. Not on a living human.

I must say that after Nan and I had grasped the situation we reacted with admirable efficiency. Nan led Magda to my office where she called the wardrobe room and told Boo to get himself upstairs on the double. I relocked the dressing room and then joined them to call the police.

Boo arrived at the office in seconds with the flask of Wild Turkey he keeps stashed in the shoe closet for emergencies. He administered a double slug to Magda, which seemed to calm her somewhat, then turned to us and demanded to know what the hell was going on. Before I could stop her, Nan gave him the highlights. I poked her in the ribs but it was too late. Boo's eyes were gleaming with unholy delight.

"Boo," I said as sternly as I could, "take Magda downstairs to the wardrobe room, and make her rest on the first-aid cot. And whatever you do don't tell Marc."

"Sugar, cross my heart and hope to die."

"Thanks," I said without conviction. Marc and Boo are partners in Gossip Central. I figured the story would be all over the building in four minutes—five tops.

After Boo left with Magda, Nan got very busy rearranging the papers on my desk. She sorted them according to size with a total disregard for content, putting them into neat little piles. It was going to take me weeks to find anything.

"I'm sorry about Boo," she said without looking up. "I just wasn't thinking."

"It probably doesn't make any difference," I said. "Everyone will know as soon as the police get here." And suddenly, as I said the word "police," the reality of what was spread out and decorated on the makeup table in Steve's dressing room hit me. And suddenly I felt very cold—the way you do when you know any minute your teeth are going to start chattering. From the desk Nan made a sound like a giggle.

"Look on the bright side," she said.

"Which is?"

"Now you don't have to go to lunch." Then she started to laugh. Calm, rational, unemotional Nan laughed until she cried—sobbed, actually—and the tears started streaming down her face. I heard someone crying with her and after a moment I realized it was me. Some toughies we were.

Chapter
Three

Going over the edge seemed to help. I wouldn't want to claim that I was in shape to win any mental health awards, but by the time the uniformed patrol guys showed up I was able to lead them to the scene of the crime without flinching. I didn't twitch when they pronounced the body dead, called for the homicide squad, and cordoned off Steve's dressing room. I just stood, kind of numb, at the doorway of the room and watched.

Seeing the homicide squad go through their drill was kind of spooky. At least once a season on our show we do a murder story and I really had to hand it to Al, our police consultant, for keeping us accurate all these years. In fact the scene in the dressing room looked so familiar that I kept waiting for one of our directors to step in and tell the cop who was taking the photographs to move a little more camera left. Except, of course, Gregg was not going to get up and walk away after we got the long shot.

There was one aspect in which life did not mirror art television-style; when the detective in charge came forward for introductions, I was not facing one of the paunchy, grizzled males we usually cast. Detective Teresa O'Hanlon was a striking redhead with a porcelain complexion and a figure any one of my actresses would have killed for. She also had a jaws-of-death handshake and an expression in her eyes which suggested that laughing wasn't her thing. Looking at her, I kicked myself for being a sexist and made a mental note to have a chat with our casting department the next time we did a cop story.

Detective O'Hanlon might not have been amused, but the situation was definitely providing entertainment for the rest of the squad.

"Ooh, sweetie," lisped a beefy specimen of our city's finest as he carefully detached Gregg's rose and bows. "This is some kinky shit. Where have you been sticking it, doll?"

"Faggots," chuckled his colleague who was holding what looked like a plastic baggie. "You gotta give 'em credit for being artistic."

"Well, Susie here must have been a real artist to make somebody this mad," said the first as he dropped the rose into the baggie.

Given Gregg's aggressive brand of heterosexuality I felt that somebody should set the record straight, but before I could say anything, the medical examiner stepped forward and started poking his finger into the small bloody hole in Gregg's chest, measuring the depth of it with his pinky. I had a quick need for a change of venue. I backed out into the hall for a minute.

The whole show was out there. Cast and crew. They were weirdly silent, just watching what they could glimpse of the activity in the dressing room with eyes as big as scared children's. They must have been there for some time but they were so quiet I didn't even know they'd gathered. As soon as they saw me, they all began to talk at once.

"Angie, what the hell is going on . . . ?"

"Somebody said there's a crazy fan . . ."

"It's terrorists . . ."

"Our security sucks . . ."

"I got a letter just last week; he wanted a pair of used pantyhose . . ."

". . . this wouldn't happen if we were on prime time . . ."

". . . they think this is a news studio . . ."

". . . I'm calling my agent . . ."

". . . I tell you, they're after Peter Jennings . . ."

As soon as I was sure I had recovered from the moment of truth in the dressing room I tried to reassure them.

"Listen, people," I began, "I don't know exactly what happened. There's been a . . ." I wimped out on the word "murder" ". . . an accident . . . and . . ."

"Ladies and gentlemen," a clear voice cut in from behind me. "I am Detective O'Hanlon. We'll need your cooperation in clearing this hallway. After that we'll be asking each of you a few questions, so don't anybody leave the building." Then she grabbed my arm and led me away, while a cop whose name tag read "P. Gonzales" began clearing a pathway through the crowd so two other cops could wheel out a gurney bearing a black plastic-covered mound which had to be Gregg's body. They bumped a little going over the doorsill and the thing on the gurney seemed to heave. I found myself grabbing for air. There were a few touches of reality Al had forgotten to include in our t.v. crime scenes.

"Are you all right, Ms. DaVito?" asked Detective O'Hanlon.

"Just peachy," I mumbled through gasps.

"Good," she said without cracking a smile. "Now, I'll need a roster of everyone who works on your show and a room where we can question them. Then I'd like to start by asking you a few . . ."

"But you can't question those people," I said, interrupting her. "We have a show to shoot."

As soon as I said it, I realized how it sounded. What I'd been thinking was that somehow once Gregg—Gregg's body—was out of the building, we'd go back to business as usual. It would be just another day in the studio, and this whole nasty murder incident would go away. One look at Detective O'Hanlon told me that my brain was on defrost.

"I guess I'd better cancel the show for today," I said.

"That would be best," said the good detective crisply.

"You can use the writers' conference room. It's right down the hall. I have to go to my office and start reworking the schedule . . ."

"Before you do that, I'd like to ask you a few questions, Ms. DaVito."

It was the way she said it that made me realize for the first time what had happened to us. Because murder isn't just about death. It's also about guilt. And suspicion. Not only was Gregg dead, each of us had become a suspect. We could be interrupted when we wanted to work, detained when we wanted to go home, questioned when we didn't want to answer. Detective O'Hanlon and her merry men would be polite, but basically the cast and crew of *Bright Tomorrow* were all potential criminals.

And what was worst of all, there would be somebody in my studio giving orders who wasn't me. It was going to be hell. This last may not have been the most appropriate thought for me to have had under the circumstances, but we megalomaniacs march to our own drummers.

Chapter
Four

The writers' office is not the tidiest room in our studio, but it does have several nice squishy pieces of furniture where our resident scribes can flop during story meetings that have gone dry.

Detective O'Hanlon chose to seat herself in the straight-backed wooden chair behind the writing desk and motioned me to pull up another equally tough-minded chair for myself. I felt the way I used to as a kid when called on the carpet for snoozing during catechism class, except that Detective O'Hanlon was much younger than Sister James Justice and she wasn't wearing a wimple. However, she did have the Nun Look down pat. That's the unblinking stare which sees straight through to your soul and knows not only every sin you've ever committed but several you're going to commit that you haven't thought of yet. I was just about to ask Teresa if she'd gone to parochial school, when she spoke.

"Tell me about this show. . . ." She checked a spiral notepad. "It's called *Bright Tomorrow,* isn't it?"

"Yes. What would you like to know? How it works? The history?"

"Start there. Give me some basic background."

"*Bright Tomorrow* is one of the old war-horse soaps. It went on the air in 1961. It's always been in the top five in the ratings, although in the last few years it's been poorly handled. In my estimation . . ." I trailed off because in my estimation it was Gregg who had handled it poorly, and suddenly I wasn't sure I wanted to say un-nice things about Gregg.

"But then I'm probably being unfair," I said, backpedaling like crazy. "This business really is a crapshoot. We do a lot of research and try to predict audience taste, but the truth is we just don't know what they'll like. Shows go through slumps. It's nobody's fault." I smiled to show what a sweet, non-hostile person I was. Teresa wrote something on her pad.

"How long have you been employed by the show, Ms. DaVito?"

"This time, about three months." The statement caught her attention.

"This time?" she repeated.

I really didn't want to get into it, but I didn't think there was any way out.

"I worked for the show before, but I quit. Artistic differences," I added, falling back on the industry's oldest cliché. Seemed to go down fine with O'Hanlon.

"And they let you come back after you quit?" she asked.

"Begged me to," I corrected.

"You must be good." I thought I saw a flicker of a smile. Teresa was probably good and knew it, too. "And exactly what were the 'artistic differences'?" she asked. She was good.

"Management wanted me to fire an actress; her name was Jesse Southland. She'd been the star of the show from the very beginning, and I felt it would be a mistake."

"So you quit?"

I nodded. Actually what I'd done was create a scandal that rocked daytime. I walked during the taping of Jesse's last show. I mean literally. I turned on my heel before her last scene and left the control booth. I went straight out of the building and refused to come back, leaving *Bright Tomorrow,* the network, the sponsor, and the advertising agency in a lurch from which they did not recover for six months. No wonder I couldn't find any work after that except kiddie specials and the Sunday morning God shows. As my agent said, it was the dumbest career move since Sylvester Stallone decided to try his hand at light comedy.

"When you say 'management' I assume you mean Gregg Whithall?" O'Hanlon brought me back to present day fast.

"Yes, Gregg, of course. And his two associates, Lucy Stone and Linda McCain. They were all a part of the decision." Which was only the technical truth because Lucy and Linda were totally under Gregg's thumb. Known as "The Girls," they really never had anything to say in the matter. It was Gregg and Gregg alone who was determined to get rid of Jesse.

Teresa was studying me, a speculative look in her eye as if she was considering her next question carefully. When there was a discreet knock at the door, I had the feeling she didn't mind the interruption.

"Come in," she said. A tall black cop with a fantastic set of dimples walked in. Like Teresa, he wasn't in uniform, which I figured meant he was a detective, but he didn't seem to be her equal in rank. He stood politely, almost at attention, until she invited him to sit.

"What do you have, Hank?" she asked.

"We've been questioning the guard. Overall security seems pretty lax, but I'd like to have a few words with Ms. DaVito."

"Of course." I jumped in before Teresa could give her permission. "But I have to tell you we're very proud of our security system, we were told it's state of the art."

Hank gave me a look of pity. "Uh huh," he said. He pulled out a pad like Teresa's and began skimming his notes.

"Now I understand there are two other shows in addition to yours that have studios in this building."

"That's right." I nodded eagerly, happy to be dealing with something I knew about. "*All My Loves* has the third and fourth floors and *Living Our Lives* is on the fifth and sixth."

"And there are executive offices on the top floor?"

"For the ABN Daytime division. That would be Gregg . . . uh . . . the Vice President in charge of Daytime, his two executive assistants, the PR people, budget, legal, and various support staffs."

"As I understand it, each two-floor unit has an internal staircase and a separate entrance."

"That's right. We're on the ground floor, so our door opens onto the lobby. Otherwise there's an elevator which stops at the third, fifth, and seventh floors."

"And on these floors the entrance locks are activated by ID cards which are issued to all employees who regularly work there."

"Yes." I was almost starting to enjoy this detecting stuff. It sure was more fun than being grilled by Teresa of the gimlet eye. "In fact, I think there's a way to get a computer printout of all the cards that have been used with the times and dates. You might want to check into it," I added helpfully.

"We've already called the security company," said Hank.

"Ah," I said. So much for Angie DaVito, girl detective.

Hank was checking his notes again. "About the floor plan, is it the same for all three studios?"

"Basically," I said. "All of the studios are two-story units. On the bottom or first floor of each unit you'll find the soundstage. It will take up most of the right side of that floor. At the back of the soundstage you'll see what looks like a large box built into the room. That's the prop room. At the other end is the control booth where the director and producer sit during taping.

"On the bottom floor you also have the wardrobe room, the hair and makeup room, and all of the actors' dressing rooms, except in our case the star dressing room, which is up here on the second floor."

"It's not that way in the other studios?"

"No. You see, *Bright Tomorrow* loses a certain amount of floor space to the building lobby. Since the star dressing room is the biggest, we had to put it on our second floor. My office is also up here, as is the rehearsal hall, the writers' room which we're in now, the actors' lounge, and the offices of the production staff."

"And there is no way someone who works on one of the other shows can get onto your floors?"

"Not without calling us and having someone buzz them in. The system is clumsy but it was set up to give us extra protection. We're very concerned about protection," I said a bit defensively. The "lax security" crack still rankled.

Hank did not pick up on it. He turned to address Teresa. "There are two problem spots," he said. "The first is down in the lobby. Anyone who has business in the building but is not a regular employee can be buzzed in by the guard at the desk. We checked his log and given the volume of the traffic during the course of a day it would be easy for anyone to slip by him."

"You don't know Charlie," I said. The two professionals exchanged a look over my head. Like parents of an unruly kid who hasn't learned not to interrupt.

"The real problem is the back entrance," Hank

continued. "I believe it's a loading dock, Ms. DaVito?"

"Yes," I said. "We store all our sets and most of the big props in warehouses in New Jersey. The trucks deliver what we need for each day's shoot to the back of the Broadcast Center in the morning. The stagehands unload them and then load them up again at the end of the workday. Since we're on the ground floor our soundstage opens directly onto the loading dock. So we just pull up our steel doors. The shows on the other floors use a freight elevator."

"And while your stagehands are loading and unloading the trucks, the entire back of the building is open to the street," said Hank.

"Yes. But trust me, it wouldn't be easy for someone to sneak in."

"Why not?" Teresa broke her silence and sat forward slightly in her chair.

"That dock is a zoo in the early morning. It's swarming with people, they're moving fast, carrying heavy furniture and set pieces. Anyone who didn't belong there would probably get trampled to death."

"But practically speaking someone could get in," she said.

"Yes. Practically speaking," I admitted. "But I don't know where they'd hide." I still wanted to defend our security system. "The soundstage is a big, open space with too many people. The prop room is out, our propmaster Tommy keeps it locked. Marc Landry and Sylvia Morris do the same with the wardrobe and hair and makeup rooms. The dressing rooms are locked, too. The actors and the wardrobe crew have keys for them. My assistant Nan Robinson unlocks all the offices on the second floor when she comes into work. Even the men's and ladies' rooms are locked until the maintenance man opens them."

Teresa was studying me again. I flashed her a big smile. It may have been a touch smug.

"So you're saying the killer couldn't have been an outsider," she said slowly. "That it had to be someone who works here."

I could feel my smile freeze. As if someone had doused me with very icy water. "No. Of course I'm not saying that. That's crazy. The people at this studio are my friends, I've known some of them for years. It's ridiculous to even suggest that one of them is a murderer."

"Ms. DaVito," said Teresa patiently, "someone did commit murder. Right here in this studio. Who do you think might have hated Gregg Whithall enough to do that?"

Now both she and Hank were studying me.

"Look," I said, squirming in my seat and thinking I should have been more careful of anyone with a Nun Look. "I don't know anything about murder and motives and that kind of thing. Gregg had a lot of power and at one time or another he probably made everybody in the studio angry. That comes with the dinner. In our business, feelings get exaggerated because we're all hambones at heart. We overstate—anything to make the story better. But it's just our style. It doesn't mean a thing."

There was a long pause, so long that if it had happened in one of my shows I'd have told the actors to tighten it up and get on with it. Then Teresa said mildly, "I think that will be all for now, Ms. DaVito. Thank you for your time. I know you have a lot of work to do." I could see Hank was as surprised as I was that she was letting me go but I didn't care. I must have set a new land speed record for jumping out of a chair and getting across a room. Ladies' division, anyway. I had the door open when Teresa stopped me. "Ms. Da-Vito," she said. "Please don't leave before you check with me. I may want to question you again."

"Sure thing," I said with a sickly smile. Great, I thought, now I have all day to stew. Which was probably the point.

Life in the studio had not stood still while I was chatting with Teresa and Hank. A frazzled Nan met me in the hallway outside my office to give me an update.

"A cop came to the office to tell me you'd decided to cancel for the day so I made an official announcement. The natives were getting restless."

"Good move," I said. "How are they now?"

"The crew is fine. Vinnie and Mitch ordered in a couple of cases of beer and everybody is down on the soundstage watching Sally Jessy Raphael on the monitors. Today's guests are lesbian transsex-

uals who cross-dress. The police let Magda go
home. She really couldn't tell them anything they
hadn't seen for themselves and she was more than
half swacked on Wild Turkey. The goddamn actors, however . . ." Nan paused to do something
which sounded a lot like grinding her teeth. ". . .
have been driving me insane. I finally threatened
to lock them in their lounge if they didn't shut up.
They're all in there now composing a letter to their
union. God, I hate actors."

"Try to think of each of them as a creative spirit
deeply in touch with the inner child."

"If it's children we want, I vote we fire the fruit
loops and bring in a bunch of talented five-year-
olds. I like five-year-olds."

"Nan, not to change the subject, but why are
we having this conversation in the hall?"

"Because your office is occupied. The Girls are
camped out in there demanding an audience."

I sighed. "Of course they are," I said. "And it's
only eleven o'clock in the morning. Will the pleas-
ures of this day never end?"

For a reply Nan opened the door to my office
with a flourish. "With your shield or upon it," she
whispered as I went in.

The Girls were seated side by side on the sofa I
never use because I hate the scratchy hundred-and-
fifty-dollar-a-yard upholstery. Physically, the
women present an interesting contrast. Lucy Stone
is slim to the point of pain. She wears aggressively
feminine designer suits, usually pink, and bundles
her bleached hair on top of her head in a messy

Gibson Girl bun. A pronounced overbite kept her from pursuing a career in performing, but she still loves to tell the actors that she considers herself one of them. She usually delivers this information to some poor son of a bitch we've just fired—excuse me, released to explore new and more exciting career opportunities.

Linda McCain is probably the prettier of the two women, but nobody ever thinks of her that way because she's so big. She's six feet if she's an inch and easily weighs in at three hundred pounds. Her eyes are a cold pale blue, her round face an impenetrable mask. It's her stillness which makes Linda so formidable. I've seen the woman sit through a four-hour story meeting without moving a muscle.

The party line is that The Girls are friends. They are said to lunch often, and I've heard rumors that they shopped for their power minks together back in the days when fur was still fun. But I've never been sure. Linda and Lucy are ambitious women who clawed their way up from the typing pool, and they both favor a slice-and-dice political style seldom seen outside small brutal dictatorships. I have a hard time imagining these Mussolinis in pantyhose as genuine pals.

When I came in they heaved themselves off my uncomfortable sofa and advanced on me. Lucy gave me an extravagant air kiss while Linda did her national monument imitation. This was standard operating procedure. Whenever they had to double-team a recalcitrant producer, Lucy was always the one to play good cop.

"Angie dear," she cooed. "How terrible for you. I heard you were the one who found him."

"Not really. It was Magda, our wardrobe mistress."

"Poor thing, and after all she's been through."

Actually no one at ABN knew Magda well enough to say what, if anything, she'd been through. However, it suits Lucy's generic form of compassion to assume that anyone who speaks with an accent must have left their homeland under dire circumstances involving great suffering. Linda continued to look at me silently.

"Angie dear, sit." Lucy ushered me into my office. Before I could protest Linda had planted herself in my comfortable armchair and Lucy hightailed it to the other side of the room, where she settled behind my desk, leaving me the sofa from hell. I think the choreography was some kind of power play meant to intimidate me. Unfortunately I'd been through a lot that morning so it just made me cranky.

"Now, we realize you were distraught." Lucy smiled her sympathy. "And we're sure you meant well . . ."

"However, we do have procedures." Linda finally gave utterance in her throaty, upper-class drawl. Linda grew up deep in the heart of Brooklyn, but whenever she speaks I automatically look around for someone named Muffy swinging a tennis racket. Sometimes I wonder about it, but at that moment I was not in the mood to speculate about Linda McCain's speech patterns.

"Would you mind telling me what this is about?" I asked crossly. "What with one thing and the other I'm not in shape to play guessing games this morning."

"You can't just take it upon yourself to cancel an entire day's shooting," Linda rumbled without moving even a minor facial muscle—a 1930s debutante with menace.

"You know better than that, Angie dear," Lucy clucked.

I couldn't believe it, they were actually giving me grief for not going through channels.

"Gee, I don't know what I could have been thinking of," I said. "There was a dead man in one of my dressing rooms, the cops were crawling all over my studio getting ready to grill everyone, and silly me, I figured that was enough reason to cancel the show."

"Angie dear, there's no need to get upset . . ." Lucy began, but I shut her off.

"Oh, I don't know." I was really warmed up now. "Finding a corpse splayed out on a makeup table can be a little upsetting, Lucy. Especially before you've had your second cup of coffee."

Lucy's voice lost its syrup. "Angie, stop it," she snapped. "I don't give a damn what kind of shock you had. Canceling a show costs the network money. You should have gone to the proper authority."

"Sorry. I thought the proper authority was dead."

There was a brief silence.

"From now on you will refer all such questions to Linda and me," said Lucy.

It took me a second, but only that, to get it. "You two are the new 'proper authority'?"

Lucy nodded. Linda inclined her head slightly. She could have been stretching her neck but I took it for a nod.

"We had a talk with the Coast," Lucy explained. They must have been on the phone before Gregg's body was out of the building. "The feeling was that we should step in in this terrible crisis."

"So the two of you are the new vice president?"

Lucy nodded again. Linda did her dip.

"When do you make the big announcement?"

Lucy started to speak, then stopped. Linda took over. "There won't be an official statement for a while," she said.

Lucy chimed in quickly, "However, there are discussions going on. Everyone knows how well Lucy and I work together. I'm sure you can appreciate how delicate the situation is, Angie dear."

"I understand," I said. And for the first time since they began their little show of force, I did.

This wasn't the first time the West Coast had contemplated a partnership in the number-one daytime slot for Lucy and Linda. The last time was seven years ago. The current vice president had just been assigned to the Elysian fields of prime time and Lucy and Linda, with twenty-two and nineteen years at the network respectively, were being considered as a team replacement.

But that was before Jesse Southland fell in love with a piranha from the ABN game show division named Gregg Whithall.

Now it seemed as if Gregg's untimely demise had turned back the clock. And this time The Girls were taking no chances. They were going to lock themselves in position so tight it would take welding equipment to get them out. And they were going to do it fast. No way anyone was going to get the chance to bring in another Gregg Whithall on them. They'd see the whole network in hell first. That included me.

"Perhaps you didn't know, Angie dear," Lucy said dreamily, "that it was the network people who insisted that Gregg bring you back on *Bright Tomorrow*. When he started having so much trouble with the show they felt maybe it was because he didn't have enough experience with it. But goodness, gracious . . ." She paused for effect. "No one could ever say that Linda and I don't have enough experience. Why, we've been here forever."

"We both worked on *Bright Tomorrow* when it was number one," Linda added.

Lucy released a tinkly laugh. "What we're trying to say, Angie dear, is that we know how terribly, terribly gifted you are but sometimes talent alone isn't enough. Sometimes we have to prove we can be part of a team."

Not a subtle message but definitely heartfelt. Once I would have argued with them, but I've gotten wise in my old age. Or maybe I've just turned chickenshit.

"I'm sorry if I was out of line canceling the show," I muttered.

"It's all right, dear," said Lucy. "That's why we wanted to have this little talk. Just so you understand that things are going to be different around here."

"Now that we're in charge," Linda added. And suddenly, because she couldn't help it, she smiled. I'd never seen Linda do that before. It made her look positively human.

Lucy couldn't keep herself from smiling either. "It's going to be such a fun time for everybody," she said. Clearly neither one of these women would be joining any grief groups for the late Gregg Whithall. But then who would? Certainly none of the people working in my studio. That thought made me shudder.

"Look," I said, "I'm afraid since I did cancel the show, I really need to get to work on rescheduling . . ."

"Of course, Angie dear, now that we've had our little talk." Lucy was back to coos and gurgles.

"Just remember, we expect to have input," Linda warned as they headed for the door.

"We're there for you, Angie dear," said Lucy as a parting shot. "From now on we at ABN are going to be one big happy family."

"Great," I said. Just what I needed, more family.

* * *

The rest of the day passed without incident. Nan made about two million phone calls to agents, managers, and union reps giving them the bad news about extra hours and the good news about overtime paychecks for their clients and members. I thought about calling our head writer Larry so he could be on point if we needed rewrites. But Larry works at home. I can handle working with Larry in the studio but calling him at home is something else. There's always the chance that Mrs. Lawrence Curtis Bradley III, also known as Chrissie— or The Idiot if you're talking to one of my friends—will answer. Because she lives there. And shares Larry's life. And his bed.

I didn't call Larry.

When five-thirty rolled around, I let Nan go home. I didn't want to leave until the intruders were off my turf, so I stayed and did paperwork. Finally when I'd cleaned up everything on my desk, including a letter of regret to the invitation committee of an acting school in New Rochelle, I looked through the window in my office door and saw Hank and three of his compadres walking wearily toward the stairs. The cops were packing it in. At last.

It took me three tries to put on my coat. I was at that stage of tired where you're too far gone to feel it. You just have a vague sense that your motor responses aren't all they should be and you might start telling long stories with no point if you could find anyone to listen. It also dawned on me that now that the cops had gone, I was all alone in a place where someone had recently been shot to death. That was why, when there was a knock at the door, my heart did one of those little dance numbers that remind you that it's been two or three years since you last had a physical.

"Yeah, what do you want?" I growled in the most forbidding tone I could muster.

In walked Teresa O'Hanlon looking as fresh as a daisy after seven straight hours of questioning strangers.

"Good, you remembered I asked you not to leave," she said. Actually I'd completely forgotten but I managed a virtuous smirk.

"So, have you finished?" I asked, trying to project "go home" vibes.

They were lost on Teresa, who sat down in my armchair. "Finished for today," she said.

"It has been a long one," I tried.

Teresa settled back. "It's just the beginning, I'm afraid."

I gave it another shot. "Well, tomorrow's another day."

Teresa didn't budge. "Tomorrow I'll be interviewing the rest of your actors," she said chattily. "I gather they don't all work every day."

I gave up. Obviously we were going to talk. I went back to my desk, turned on the lamp, and sat. "No, the entire cast doesn't work every day. On a soap we run five or six different stories simultaneously, each involves different characters, and we don't play all the stories every day."

"So I understand. Ms. DaVito, I wanted to ask you . . ."

"Look, would you mind calling me Angie? 'Ms. DaVito' makes me think of my great-aunt Graziella who always wears black to family weddings."

I wouldn't want to say that the request shattered her poise, Teresa O'Hanlon didn't shatter. But she was thrown off guard. It took her a few seconds to process the concept, running it through her mental computer, before she finally had to decide that there was nothing against it in department regulations. "All right," she said.

I tried not to look triumphant. "Thank you."

"No problem." She gave me a warm smile. "So, Angie, tell me why you disliked Gregg Whithall so much?"

I'm not a cop trained to stay cool no matter what. I shattered. "What?" I stammered. "Who said . . . ?"

Teresa smiled again. "You did. When a woman whose whole life is her work suddenly quits without warning because she's having a conflict with her boss, I want to know the whole story. There has to be more to it than you told me."

I fiddled with a couple of knickknacks on my desk. Then I figured, what the hell. She'd been questioning people all day and everyone knew the way I felt about Gregg. I hadn't exactly made a secret of it.

"Gregg Whithall was a prick. He was a user, a bully, and a no-talent."

"The lack of talent being the worst crime of all," said Teresa dryly.

I didn't laugh. "No, the worst thing about him was the way he liked to hurt people."

"How did he hurt you?"

"He made me help him kill Jesse Southland."

Teresa didn't blink. "Kill?" she asked mildly.

"As good as." I paused for a moment, trying to decide where to start. "When you were a kid, did you ever watch *Bright Tomorrow*? When you were home with the flu or something?"

She shook her head apologetically and I realized what a dumb question it was. Teresa O'Hanlon never got sick. She was the girl who got the perfect attendance award for all twelve years when she graduated from high school.

"Well, in the early days Jesse Southland was *Bright Tomorrow*. I don't just mean she was the star, I mean the show was her empire. She was so popular she could get almost anything she wanted from the network."

"And she enjoyed her power."

"She reveled in it. And she did a lot of good with it. At least from my point of view."

"Was she responsible for getting you your job with the show?"

"Jesse was responsible for my entire career. When I first met her, I was still trying to be an actress. All I could get was extra work but Jesse saw to it that they called me for *Bright Tomorrow* whenever they needed a warm body. I think she knew how much I needed the money, but she said it was because I could stand next to her in a crowd scene without making her look like a dwarf. I'm only five foot one so Jesse had almost three-quarters of an inch on me. She liked that a lot."

"Yes," said Teresa thoughtfully. "I had the feeling she was a small woman. There was something fragile about her. Very striking, of course, with that pale hair and those blue eyes—almost lavender, weren't they?"

"I thought you said you never watched the show," I said.

"No, I never have. But I did see a picture of Miss Southland today. One of your people showed it to me. A little gray-haired man. He's head of your property department, I think."

"Tommy Props. I didn't know he had a picture of Jesse."

"Actually, he has two. One he keeps in the desk in his prop room—I believe that one is a publicity picture—and a small snapshot he keeps in his wallet."

"How did you find out?" I demanded, fascinated and a little pissed because she knew something about one of my troupe that I didn't.

"It is my job to ask questions . . . and to find out what I need to know."

"Which you always do?" I wasn't being too petty.

"Always," she responded serenely. "Please go on with your story."

I thought about refusing, just to show her that she couldn't always find out what she needed to

know, but I figured if I gave her a rough time it
might seem as if I had something to hide. Besides,
I found I wanted to talk. The building around us
was silent, my office was dark except for the light
from my desk lamp, and I was tired but revved.

Teresa relaxed even deeper into the armchair,
giving me the kind of easy attention you get from
a good friend. Later I realized that the notebook
was nowhere in sight.

"I was twenty years old and I was drowning. I'd
been a kid performer but I hadn't aged well. I
knew I wanted to stay in show business but I
didn't know how. One day when I was working
the show, Jesse pulled me into her dressing room
to have lunch. I'd run out of money the day before
so I was hungry. Jesse watched me inhale everything edible except her breath mints and then she
said, 'Lovey, I've decided to fix your life. You're
not an actor. You have the taste and the passion,
but not the ego. You'd never walk into a friend's
hospital room, see that she has three guests, and
think, Thank God, an audience. So I'm going to
make you the executive producer of *Bright Tomorrow*. You'll have to learn the ropes, of course,
but that won't be a problem for you. I've been
wanting to have a woman at the helm for some
time now and you're my golden opportunity.
You'll start tomorrow.' And the next day I was
working on the show in the production office."

"Just like that?"

"In those days you didn't fight with Jesse Southland. She may have been small but she had the

soul of a Mack truck. Sort of like Napoleon."

"Or Hitler. Why did it all fall apart for her? What happened?"

"I'd like to say Gregg Whithall happened, but it was more complicated than that. About seven years ago Jesse hit a crisis. She was well into her forties and it was starting to show. It wasn't a problem on the show yet, she was still the empress, but she knew the clock was ticking. She had a few nips and tucks, she changed her hairstyle, but she was still running scared. And Jesse didn't know how to cope with being scared. She'd always been fearless.

"When she met Gregg at the network Christmas party she was ripe for an affair. He didn't even have to work to get her. He was a few years younger, good-looking . . ."

"If you like the type," Teresa murmured. I think she surprised herself as much as she did me because she flushed ever so slightly. "I'm trained to be observant. Excuse me."

"That's okay, I don't go for beauties like Gregg Whithall either."

"But Jesse Southland did."

"She was mad for him. I don't know if Jesse had ever been in love like that before. She'd always been so involved with her career. But she made up for it with Gregg. Whatever he wanted he had to have. And he wanted to be Vice President of Daytime at ABN."

"And she managed to get it for him? Without him learning the ropes?"

"Gregg did have a bit of a track record. He'd been successful with a couple of game shows and a few people thought that maybe that was the wave of the future for daytime. And to give the devil his due, the man did give great lunch. But you're right, Jesse went to the mat for him big time.

"After he got the job, things rocked along for about a year. He didn't know the first thing about soap opera, but Jesse did and she coached him. The lineup was healthy and the Coast was happy. Then Jesse found out that he was sleeping with another woman. And that he'd been cheating on her from the very beginning, even back when she was putting her career on the line for him."

Teresa didn't say anything but her eyes sparkled with the same mix of anger and pity I'd seen in other women when I told the story. I guess I'd told it so often because it bothered me so much.

"Jesse was wild when she found out. She tried to get Gregg fired but it was too late. She'd built him too well, and besides, she was finally starting to slip. We'd introduced several new characters on the show and they were beginning to take off. I was exec-producing by then and I tried to warn her. But Jesse wouldn't understand. She couldn't. She went on waging her war and, eventually . . ."

I couldn't sit still anymore. I got out of my chair and went to look out my window. I have a snazzy view of the building next door. "I tried to protect her," I said softly to the brick wall.

But had I? When it would have done some

good? Before the new characters started crowding her out? But they were Larry's characters and he loved them like his children.

And we were having so much fun working together, doing it so well. *Bright Tomorrow* was the hottest show in daytime. Larry and I were the hottest team. To say nothing of being hot for each other.

"It took Gregg six months and a hell of a lot of lunch to get the okay from the brass to fire Jesse, but he got it. I tried to fight him, but I didn't have the clout."

Or the backup from Larry who, as head writer, would have been a powerful ally.

"Gregg could have fired her himself, but he knew how I felt about Jesse, so he made me do it. He enjoyed setting up scenarios like that.

"On the day I had to tell her, Gregg had security remove her things from the star dressing room and lock the door. Jesse refused to let me take her to my office so I had to fire her in the hallway."

There's just so long you can stare at a brick wall before you start seeing patterns that aren't there. I turned away from the window. But I didn't feel like sitting again. I began to circle the room. Eventually I wound up in front of the shelf where I keep the trophy the *Bright Tomorrow* cast won when they did the celebrity play-offs on *Family Feud*. At the time, saving it had seemed funny.

"After she left *Bright Tomorrow*, Jesse went out to prove she could still work. She called everyone she knew in the industry. But she was too identified with Claire Wingate, her character on the show. And she was holding out for a lead. She just couldn't seem to grasp that she wasn't a leading lady anymore.

"She never spoke to me again, but I kept track as well as I could. Then I heard that she . . . Well, I'm sure someone you talked to today told you that Jesse died two years ago in a car crash."

Teresa nodded. "It was out in the Midwest, wasn't it?"

"Ohio. She was doing dinner theater in a shopping mall. All the ham and roast beef you could eat, plus Jesse Southland, for eleven ninety-five.

"The general manager of the theater contacted Tommy Props and told him. He was the only one Jesse had stayed in touch with during those years. I think they found his phone number in her purse.

"So that's how it ended for Jesse. With a phone call from a stranger to a man who had never addressed her as anything but Miss Southland." My earlier weariness was back with a vengeance. I looked wistfully at the door. But Teresa wasn't moving.

"Wasn't there some sort of party . . . ?"

If there was one thing I didn't want to talk about it was that lousy party.

"Look, if you've heard all of this . . ."

"I haven't heard it from you."

"The party was one of Jesse's grandstand plays that didn't make it. It was the timing mostly. I mean, there we were, a couple of weeks after we'd heard she'd driven herself into an embankment, trying to do a cut from an old MGM show biz movie—toast Jesse with champagne, and sing a few choruses of 'There's No Business Like Show Business' in her memory. We just couldn't pull it off."

"Why do you say it was Ms. Southland's grandstand play?"

"Because it was her idea. She'd left three thousand dollars in her will with instructions to poor old Tommy Props that all her pals were to go to Sardi's and have dinner on her one last time. Jesse loved picking up the check."

"Sounds like a nice way to celebrate a life."

"If you felt like celebrating."

"None of you did?"

"We were angry."

"Who in particular?"

"Everybody. If you're fishing for Gregg's murderer, forget it. We all went around muttering his name under our breath like it was a curse."

"You blamed him that much?"

She was starting to get on my nerves.

"Detective, Jesse didn't just love her work, it was the way she defined herself. She was Jesse Southland, the actress—the star of *Bright Tomorrow*. When that was taken away from her, it was as if . . ." That was a thought I really didn't want to finish. "Jesse couldn't live without *Bright Tomorrow* and thanks to Gregg, I'm the one who stood in that fucking hallway and took it away from her."

I finished my tour of the room and flopped

down in my chair again. I glared at Teresa defiantly.

"And that does not mean that I killed the son of a bitch, just that I would have liked to. Which merely puts me about midway on a very long list."

I imagine one of the many skills a good cop should have is the ability to know when the interview is over. For the first time since we'd started talking, Teresa sat upright and pulled out her notebook. No more warm fuzzies, Detective O'Hanlon was back on duty. She wrote briefly, then looked up at me.

"I'm sorry if I've kept you," she said. "You must be tired." She started to put the notebook away, then she seemed to think of something. "One more thing," she said. "Can you think of any reason why a Mr. . . . ." She checked her notes. ". . . Lawrence Bradley should have used his ID card to enter this building last night at eleven o'clock?"

Larry had been at the studio? At eleven o'clock at night? Larry was usually in bed by eleven o'clock. He liked to get to his computer before eight in the morning and he had to have an hour of solitude first. It was one of the things that used to drive me crazy about him in the days when we were still driving each other crazy.

"Are you sure?" I asked. Naturally Teresa the Infallible was sure but I was stalling for time. The ramifications of this were dawning on me fast, and I wanted to feel my way.

"We have the computer printout for the entire

day," she said. "Mr. Bradley was the last person to enter the building. Have you any idea what he might have been doing here?"

Before I could answer her the phone rang. I picked it up.

"Angie, I've been trying to get you at home for an hour. What the hell are you doing at the office?" It was Larry.

It isn't true that your heart stops when you have a sudden scare. The most it does is miss a few beats. But other things do happen. You feel sort of weightless, the way you do when you've tripped but you haven't yet started to fall. And your brain goes into slow motion. Which is why it took me a couple of decades to finally say, "Why, hello there, how are you?"

"Angie?" Larry sounded nervous. "You're not alone, are you? Are the police there? Just answer yes or no."

"Why, yes," I chirped, trying not to look at Teresa, who was watching me with what I hoped was idle curiosity.

"Get out of there as fast as you can," Larry said. "I'll meet you at your apartment."

"What a terrific idea," I said, still doing the bird thing. "First thing tomorrow morning. Say eight-ish?"

"No, now. I've got to see you, Angie." The last time the man said those words to me over a phone it was three o'clock in the morning, I was in bed naked, and he was urging me to throw on a coat with nothing else and get over to his apartment on the double. But that was five years ago. Five years, a wife, and now a murder. Only a glutton for punishment would have agreed to what he was asking.

"Okay," said the candidate for Masochist of the Year. "Thanks so much for calling." And I hung up.

I searched my brain wildly for some explanation to give Teresa, but she seemed to have lost interest in me. She stood up and stretched ever so slightly. "My, what a long day this has been," she said. "Thank you for your cooperation."

"Well, I just hope I was able to help," I said. Now I was sounding the way Mary Tyler Moore used to sound when she talked to Mr. Grant. I had to get the hell out of there. "I'll just close up and we can be on our way."

Teresa waited while I quickly packed up my briefcase, collected my coat, and turned out the light. We walked in silence together through the hallway, down the stairs, and out to the lobby. As we passed through the lobby door she paused. "I can't help wondering . . ." she said.

Swell, I thought. I should have known eventually we'd talk about that damn phone call. "What about?" I asked carefully.

"I wonder who the woman was. The one who was having the affair with Gregg Whithall."

I shifted gears with relief. "I don't think Jesse ever knew her name. But whoever she was, she was part of a crowd."

"I'm sure." We were at the entrance. Teresa stuck out her hand for me to shake. "Good night, Ms. . . ." For a second I thought "DaVito" was going to slip out, but she caught herself. "Good night," she repeated, neatly sidestepping the entire issue. I gathered we weren't on a first-name basis after all. We shook hands solemnly. Then we took off in different directions.

The weather had turned; there was a sharp nip in the air.

Chapter
Five

My apartment building is one of the few on the Upper West Side that couldn't muster enough Yuppies to turn co-op during the greed boom of the eighties. But that's not the only reason I love it. It has a nice beat-up feeling that reminds me of my youth when I was poor and hopeful and my local greasy spoon did not serve sun-dried tomatoes or goat cheese.

My apartment is fairly funky, too. Maybe I should grow up, or at least buy a copy of *Apartment Living* and check out the decorating tips, but the truth is, I like it the way it is. On one wall is the bookcase where I keep the leather-bound copies of playbills from every show I've ever seen. Next to the bookcase is the shelf with the scrapbooks of my older sister Connie and me in the early days when Mama was booking weekend gigs for our act in the better Elks Clubs and American Legion Posts of Connecticut and New Jersey.

I've kept most of the furniture I scavenged off the streets when I first started living on my own, as well as the thrift shop specials, although a few years ago I did have everything refinished and upholstered. On my sofa I have five of the teddy bears Connie and I collected from our fans during the winter when we were regulars on Uncle Beano's radio show, and the big rag doll Uncle Beano gave me for Christmas. And I have lots of tables. Mostly little tables with long skirts that I cover with all the framed photographs and souvenirs and stuff I have. I'm very fond of my stuff.

My kitchen is where I make coffee.

But best of all I love my bedroom. As soon as I was hired full time on *Bright Tomorrow*, I bought myself a canopy bed. Then one weekend the set designer from the show and I swagged it with yards of black velvet he had left over from a fantasy sequence and filled a large brass urn with black and white plumes from the same event. Over the years I've added other amenities like rugs, drapes, chests of drawers, and a cushy chaise, but I keep replacing the swags and the plumes just the way they were. Larry said sleeping in my bed was like being in a DeMille movie about Elizabeth the First. He didn't seem to mind it, though—not then.

But this was now. The Larry who was coming over to my apartment was a different person. He was a professional colleague, my head writer. Nothing more to me than a respected co-worker. Said I to myself.

I hit the front door of my apartment at a dead run. I didn't really have time for a shower but I decided on a fast one anyway. I like the way I feel after a shower and if I use the scented soap it makes the apartment smell sexy.

After my shower I spent several precious minutes rummaging through my lingerie. I'm a fairly conservative dresser, never really having had the confidence to stray too far away from good labels and things that match. But when it comes to my lingerie I go a little crazy. I have a thing for lace and satin and thin French silk with lots of trim and tiny rosettes. In addition to black, I'm partial to colors with names like Jewel Blue and Raspberry Ice.

After some debate I finally settled on the Sea Foam Green lace panties and bra which do wonders for my eyes, although of course they wouldn't tonight because no one was going to see them except me. I pulled on a pair of gabardine slacks and a silk blouse and went into the bathroom to repair my face. I'm much better-looking than I used to be. When I was a kid the whole family agreed that I was the spitting image of my Uncle Paulie the bookie. Fortunately when Uncle Paulie died he left me a small inheritance which I promptly invested in a nose job. I knew Paulie would have understood. Now as long as I keep my weight down I look okay. Maybe even a little better than okay.

The doorbell rang just as I was applying my second coat of mascara. I ran so fast to answer it that I didn't have time to think until the door was open and Larry was there. Standing in the hall outside my door. Just the way he used to. There are times when your heart can stop after all.

We stood there looking at each other. I don't think either of us knew what to do. Larry tried a smile but his face flushed dark pink; I was having trouble getting my tongue free from the roof of my mouth.

It was so stupid. We'd been working together every day since I came back on the show. We talked to each other with no problem; every once in a while we even argued. But that was work. This was my apartment. Which was also Memory Lane.

Finally he got it together enough to say "Hi" and I managed, "Come on in," which got us through the door.

He walked around reacquainting himself with the place while I watched him. He was wearing his uniform: faded jeans, the shetland sweater he shouldn't have put in the washer in 1974, and the ratty tweed jacket that used to belong to his father. He gets away with this ensemble because he has never cared what anyone else thinks. It's not arrogance, it's just what happens when the summer place on the Vineyard has been in your family since before rocks and there were three buildings at your prep school named after your ancestors.

I don't know if anyone else would think he's handsome. His face is too thin and his eyes are too deep-set; lighting them for camera would be a nightmare. But they're great eyes, gray-blue and fringed with lashes so thick they look unreal. He has streaky blond hair that looks like he does a lot of sunshine sports except that he hates the outdoors, and long, lean muscles he doesn't deserve given the way he avoids all forms of exercise. And I'm a sucker for his smile. Correction, I used to be.

"Would you like some coffee?" I asked. "I'm

afraid I don't have any beer." Larry's beverage of choice is any beer that hasn't been imported or brewed with mountain spring water.

"That's okay. I don't drink much beer anymore," he said. "We started working out and . . ." He stopped abruptly. No doubt who the other half of "we" was. "Damn it, Ange," he burst out, "I'm sorry about this. I shouldn't have come. But I need your help . . ."

That broke the spell for me. "No problem," I said. "Please sit down. And since we're having this chat, what the hell were you doing in the studio last night at eleven o'clock?"

He looked at me as if I'd just sprouted a second head. "Oh Jesus," he said. "How did you find out?"

"A very smart cop named O'Hanlon told me. Detective Teresa O'Hanlon. I imagine you'll be meeting her soon."

"Tomorrow. At noon, in her office at the precinct. Shit." He started to pace.

I chose my next words carefully. "Larry, I don't know what's going on with you. And I'm not sure I want to know. But Teresa O'Hanlon is no fool. You'll be better off telling her the truth, no matter how bad it is."

He stopped mid-pace and stared at me, then he laughed. "Ange, cut the melodrama. I didn't kill Gregg."

"Glad to hear it. But someone did."

That sobered him fast. "I went to the studio last night to talk to Gregg."

He was lying. I knew it because I knew him. I wasn't sure I wanted to know why he was lying. Larry moved a couple of the teddy bears and sat on the sofa.

"Gregg set the time," he said. "He had some kind of late meeting at the studio. We were supposed to meet in the writers' office, but when I arrived he wasn't there."

He'd rehearsed every word he was saying. I'd seen him do it dozens of times before, whenever we were going to pitch a difficult story to the network. "Just glide by the tricky stuff and lay out the plot points nice and slow," he'd say. It was an effective technique if you didn't know what he was doing.

"I looked for Gregg," he continued. "But he wasn't anywhere in the studio. I checked both floors. Then I hung around for a few more minutes until I got tired of waiting and I left. After I got home, I called his office and his apartment but he wasn't in either place. I figured maybe his mysterious meeting was a late date that had turned into an all-nighter. So I went to bed. Then this morning Nan calls me and tells me Gregg was killed last night. I've been going crazy all day wondering what the hell was going on over at the studio."

"Why didn't you call and ask?"

"With the police all over the place? Ange, I was in the fucking building last night. It could have been happening while I was there. I didn't hear anything, but the sound could have been muffled a hundred different ways, I've laid out enough murder plots to know that. I also know I could be in a hell of a lot of trouble. That's why I wanted to see you before I talk to the police tomorrow. I need you to fill me in."

It was a good job, the plot points were nicely laid out, you almost couldn't see the gliding. But I knew him.

"What was so important that you had to talk about it at eleven o'clock at night?" I asked.

He looked down at his hands and twisted his wedding band a couple of times. I've always wondered how The Idiot conned him into wearing jewelry. Then he looked back at me. "I knew you were going to ask that. I can't tell you. But I swear it has nothing to do with what happened. Just trust me, Ange, please."

I hated how scared he was. But he was living in a dream world if he thought any of us would be keeping any secrets about anything from now on.

"I want to know, Larry," I said.

It took him a few seconds. "I went over there to tell him to stay away from my wife," he said.

I should have said something tactful. Or sympathetic. At the least I should have kept quiet. I laughed. First I was speechless, then I started to roar. Larry didn't say a word. He just got to his feet and headed for the door.

I grabbed his arm. "Larry, it came at me out of left field, give me a break," I said. But I couldn't sound contrite because I was enjoying myself too much.

And Larry knew I was. He disentangled his arm gently. "Ange, coming here tonight was stupid and selfish. And you have every right to haul out the machetes and have a high old time. But I don't feel like sticking around for the fun. Even if I do deserve it. So I'm going home. Thanks for warning me about the detective."

I wasn't going to beg him to stay. I walked him to the door. He started to open it, but he couldn't go just yet.

"By the way," he said, "they weren't sleeping together. And she never did anything to encourage him." He looked at me and he tried to grin. "And you're thinking if I buy that, there's a nifty bridge in Brooklyn you want to sell me."

I shook my head. "Beachfront property in Nebraska."

"I believe her, Ange."

"Why?"

"Because I love her."

"Whatever for?" It slipped out. I swear.

"Oh, I don't know, Ange, maybe because she's never called me a ball-less wonder."

"You can't count that. We were fighting."

"For a change."

"We didn't fight that much."

"Jesus."

"Okay, we fought a lot. Everybody fights."

"Ange, you fight. In your family a blood feud can start over the right way to make tomato sauce.

The rest of us aren't like that."

"Well, forgive us peasants."

"That's not what I meant."

"It was a snotty thing to say."

"I'm just trying to point out that not everyone wants to live in the last act of *La Traviata*."

"Actually the last act of *La Traviata* is rather quiet. You really should check your references."

"Speaking of snotty."

We stood there, breathing hard, glowering at each other. There was a time when my next move would have been to kiss him. But he pulled his lips into that thin line that I hate and turned away.

"This is crazy," he muttered. "I don't have to do this anymore." And he stalked out.

That night I slept better than I had in months.

Chapter
Six

The reason I continue to use a human answering service is I need the morning wake-up calls. Having spent my formative years traipsing through New England with the Italian Mama Rose, I now have the biorhythms of a bat and any hour before noon is the middle of the night to me. The operators at StarsAnserFone know that they may not hang up until I have proved that I know the day of the week, the country in which I am living, and my entire name.

However, the morning after Gregg's murder I woke, wide-eyed and alert, an hour before my call. My mind seemed to have gone into overdrive while I was sleeping and it was working frantically to focus on something. Something which I knew or should have known. Something which might have had some bearing on the murder if only I could have thought of it. I hate the kind of vague stuff my mind comes up with when I'm sleeping.

I wasted about five minutes lying in bed staring at the underside of my canopy, trying to force whatever it was to make the trip from my right brain to my left brain—or wherever the hell it is you want your thoughts to be so you can use them—but finally I gave up in disgust.

I spent a few more minutes pondering the phony story Larry had tried to sell me about his high jinks in the studio. I reviewed the whole saga, looking for holes the way we do with our long stories before we pitch them to network. I came up with a beaut. Which, I promised myself, would be discussed before the day was over.

Then, mission accomplished, I lounged back on my pillows and thought about Larry. And the way I'd felt, seeing him in my apartment again. I let myself wonder if he'd told The Idiot where he was going. And spent some pleasurable time imagining her reaction. At which point I realized it was definitely time to get up.

I hauled myself out of bed, flicked on the t.v., which is a reflex action for me in the morning, and headed in the general direction of the bathroom. A familiar voice stopped me before I got halfway across the room.

"In spite of this tragedy, Ms. Stone and I want to assure our viewers that ABN Daytime will continue—under its new management—to bring them the high-quality programming they have come to expect." I turned to the t.v. as first Linda, then Lucy came on screen. They were giving a live interview in front of the Broadcast Center.

Linda was displaying an unexpected star quality. Her hair was the kind that catches the light on camera. Her face glowed rosily in the early morning cold. Lucy, on the other hand, was shivering uncontrollably. Also, for reasons known only to herself and her God, she'd chosen to wear a turban—in the same shade of pink as the tiny smear of lipstick on her left front tooth.

"Because of the extreme pressure under which our people work, we are not allowing the press inside the Broadcast Center at this time. However, Ms. Stone and I do understand that this crime is of great interest to the public and we will make ourselves available to reporters to give updates as new developments occur." Linda flashed a Miss America smile. Where the hell did that come from?

I flicked to another channel. Only to discover a taped interview with Linda and Lucy done the previous evening in a local studio. Same thing on the other two sunrise news shows. The message was always the same: Lucy Stone and Linda McCain were now in charge of ABN, they and they alone would be talking to the press. Exhibiting in this manner their control of the situation to some very important people to whom control was very important. The Girls had been busy, bless their hearts.

I realized just how serious The Girls' stranglehold was when I got to the Broadcast Center about forty-five minutes later. Stationed at the front doors were three burly private security guards. They were doing their macho best to be menacing in spite of the fact that they were dressed in the ABN uniform, a pretty little confection designed for the network by a costumer with a fetish for *The Student Prince*.

Several reporters hovered nearby, minicams and cameras at the ready. Whenever anyone approached the Broadcast Center the contingent from Old Vienna raced to escort them inside, smoothly cutting out the folk from the press who were reduced to shouting their questions into the air. The guards were good. It was not their fault that they looked like they were about to break into a chorus of "The Drinking Song."

Inside the lobby, Teresa's cops were in charge of security. And all hell was breaking loose. A long line of ABN employees snaked back and forth like a bank line where the decorator forest had been. Checkpoint Charlie had also been dismantled. In its place two polite but determined cops were checking everyone's IDs. Charlie stood off to the side glowering. The ABN troops were not happy either.

"You don't seem to understand," Richard Ruskin, the director for *All Our Loves,* was shouting. "I am late for my rehearsal. There are actors waiting for me. I have never kept my actors waiting in a thirty-two-year career."

The cops paid no attention to that or similar pleas coming from other parts of the line. I sighed and took my place behind Tommy Props' assistant Nate, who happened to be last in line.

"How long have you been waiting?" I asked.

"About ten minutes. They're moving pretty fast. I saw Vinnie go in already. And most of his crew. One of the cops tipped him off yesterday that this might happen so he gave everyone an early call."

"Swell," I said and began trying to calculate my overtime budget in my head. Nate smiled nervously.

"Uh, Angie," he began, then he looked away. "I heard . . . well, somebody said that Gregg's body was, well, that there was a flower . . ."

I wanted to tell him everything—I would have done it in perfect deadpan. But I'm the boss. And that translates to adult. Which means I don't spread stories which could have a negative impact on my show. No matter how funny they may be.

"I understand a gold lamé rose was found at the scene of the crime," I said primly.

Nate's reaction was amazing. He went white. Literally. I thought he might pass out.

"A gold rose? Are you sure?" he croaked. Then he looked at me and made a visible effort to pull himself together. "I mean, well, you know, this thing is terrible, isn't it? I mean, for Gregg, the poor son of a bitch."

Which was really strange coming from Nate, who was devoted to Tommy and had hated Gregg for the way he terrorized the little guy.

"Look, Nate . . ." I began. But he whirled around and turned his attention to the front of the line.

"What is this shit?" he demanded savagely. "Are they going to keep us here all day?"

As I stared at the back of his head I remembered the moment when I first realized that we were all suspects. And once again I had that same vague, uneasy feeling I'd had when I awakened.

Teresa's guys were thorough but efficient. In twenty minutes Nate and I were through the line and in the studio. We both raced to the soundstage door, then stopped short, jaws dropped, gaping at the scene in front of us.

It looked as if somebody had replaced our chaotic crew with a bunch of well-programmed robots. Two stagehands hoisted a heavy couch in perfect unison, and, after neatly sidestepping a cameraman who was checking his shot cards, deposited their burden square on its marks without dropping it once. A carpenter stood back politely from the set he was fixing so a painter could touch up a flat. And it was quiet. No one was yelling. Except for the occasional muttered "'Scuse me," no one was even talking. Mitch's lighting crew was murmuring into their walkie-talkies. Every once in a while the sound of hammering broke the hush, but that was about it. It was downright spooky.

After I got over my shock, I noticed that the huge, garage-style metal door at the back of the soundstage was down. This door comprises the back wall of our soundstage and opens onto the loading dock. In the mornings it is raised so that our crews can carry in whatever we've ordered from the Jersey warehouse. After that day's set has been hauled in, the door is lowered while we shoot the show. It isn't raised again until after we finish shooting. Then the crews reload the trucks and return everything to the warehouse. But this morning the door was down, effectively closing off the loading dock and the outside world. Even the small door next to it was closed. And four of Vinnie's biggest stagehands seemed to be missing. Tiptoeing so as not to disturb anyone, I made my way to the back of the soundstage, opened the small side door, and stepped out onto the dock to investigate.

There were four more cops stationed at the street entrance of the loading dock, ready to check the IDs of anyone who wanted to come in. A disgruntled reporter was being turned away politely but firmly. Clearly the police intended to patrol the back of the Broadcast Center as well as the front.

Given the fact that three hour-long soaps used this dock and all three unloaded for their shows at the same time, the security measures imposed by the police should have created havoc. But a master intelligence seemed to have been at work. Silent and efficient crews from each of the shows were unloading into neat groupings which seemed to have been arranged show by show and set by set. Near me, Vinnie and his two counterparts from the other two soaps were huddled in earnest conference with Hank.

"So we each keep the same four guys out here every day for the loading and the unloading," Vinnie was saying. "That way, Sergeant, your guys will get to recognize them, and if anyone else tries to get in the building by giving you a load of bull about being on one of the crews, you'll know they're lying. We keep the elevators and the studio door closed until we've got a full dock, then we open up the building and bring the stuff in while you watch." He caught my eye and smiled. "Hey,

Angie," he said cheerily, "we're having a little lo-gistical problem here."

"Looks to me like you've got it knocked. This is amazing, Vinnie."

I think he actually blushed. "Yeah, well, the Ser-geant here and his men are gonna be around until they figure out this shit. So we hadda work out something. No fucking big deal," he added mod-estly, thereby supporting my personal theory that any good studio crew chief could run General Mo-tors if he had the right wardrobe. Although these days, I'm not sure Vinnie would see that as a com-pliment.

Upstairs things were also weirdly quiet. At first I thought the hallway was deserted. But as I began the trek to my office, two figures materialized at my side. They were Elizabeth ("Just call me Bitsy") Dowers and her son Jeffy. Jeffy is a child actor who plays a crucial part in one of our storylines. As kids in the profession go, he's a real find, never having forgotten a line or stage direction in his five-year career. I try not to think about the fact that Bitsy drills his dialogue into his head by using training techniques that have been outlawed by the Society for the Prevention of Cruelty to Animals.

Several months ago Bitsy herself had been out-lawed from the building by Gregg. The ban had been a serious impediment to the campaign of non-stop ass kissing she considers so vital to the advancement of Jeffy's career. Now, obviously, with the fat cat deceased, she'd decided the mouse should make up for lost time.

"You poor dear thing," she cooed at me. "I just bet you didn't sleep a wink. You could have called me. Everybody says I'm a very sympathetic listener. After all, I am a mommy."

"Gee." It was all I could think to say. Which was okay when you were talking with Bitsy.

"Jeffy was so upset, he didn't sleep a wink himself. You know how children are. And of course Jeffy's so sensitive. Not that this will interfere with our work. You can count on us. In fact I told Jeffy that today we'll just have to dedicate our performance to dear Mr. Whithall . . ."

"What a lovely thought. If you'll excuse me . . ."

"Angie." Nan rushed up and yanked me away from Bitsy, who faded off to reinforce the case for matricide with another audience. "Did you know the police were going to call in the whole cast today?"

"It's just the actors they didn't question yesterday," I soothed.

"Well, it looks like the entire goddamn membership of AFTRA. I've socked 'em away in their lounge, but don't blame me if they get out. Also, I finally tracked down Steve Robbe and ordered him to come home."

"He isn't back from his promo trip yet?"

"He decided to spend another night in beautiful downtown Cleveland. I explained that the cops are eager to meet with him because the unfortunate incident took place in his dressing room. At first he was hostile. However, I received a fax a little while ago saying that he will come here directly from the airport with his publicist, his assistant, and his masseur."

"Damn that writer from *USA Today*," I said. Ever since some besotted critic stated that our leading man had the "classy charisma of a young Cary Grant," Steve has felt it necessary to travel with an entourage.

Chapter
Seven

I decided to avoid the actors in the lounge but I did break a cardinal rule and check out the rehearsal hall. The scene being rehearsed was not wonderful. We were wrapping up our summer kid story, so the eighteen-year-old former model who talks through her nose and the gorgeous hunk who I swear is mentally challenged were meandering through yet another love scene. In the best of times these two are not Lunt and Fontanne. This morning, with all the tension in the air, they were hitting a new low.

The director, Rusty Jones, threw me a look of comic despair and pulled his ancient baseball cap even farther down over his eyes when he saw me come in. Rusty's a wily old-timer so I knew there was no way he'd let this crap go on air. By the time we taped the scene most of the dialogue would be cut and Jason, the hunk, would be shirtless and crawling all over a mercifully silent Heather. Next year both of these kids would be nominated for Best Newcomer Emmys. Watching them, it was a depressing thought.

Then suddenly the entire atmosphere in the rehearsal hall changed. Rusty sat up, Heather and Jason focused—because Anna Martin, who plays our resident bitch, had come on. With her usual power she began forcing the pace, pushing the kids until they came alive. In real life, Anna is a gentle, vague creature who lives with her mother and spends her spare time rescuing stray animals. Her outfit of choice is usually something sack-like in shades of mud, her glasses are held together with a safety pin, her pantyhose invariably have runs. It takes at least an hour and a half for the magicians in hair, makeup, and wardrobe to turn her into the chic, tough businesswoman she plays. But it's worth the time and energy because, dear God, the woman can act. She polished off the scene with the kind of pizzazz most actors only dream of, then turned to Rusty with a face of pure misery.

"I'm sorry about the monologue," she said unhappily. "I just can't seem to concentrate . . ." She stopped as she caught sight of me.

"Oh, Angie," she wailed as she rushed over to me. "It's just so terrible about Gregg, isn't it?" And then she burst into tears.

When I got back to my office I buzzed Nan and asked her to come in.

"Do you remember the time Anna found that stray mutt outside the studio and I said she could bring it inside to be safe until she left for home but then Gregg found out and overruled me and while she was pleading with him the poor little thing ran off and was killed in traffic right outside the building later that day?"

"It was not an incident to forget, why?"

"After that did Gregg do anything that you know of that might possibly have made up for it as far as Anna was concerned?"

"Are you kidding? Angie, what's gotten into you?"

"I'm just wondering what reason Anna Martin might have for weeping over Gregg Whithall."

"She doesn't. Do you want me to type something for you, or can I go back to my desk and continue hanging up on reporters?"

"What reporters?"

"Those members of the fourth estate who have managed to get past our switchboard. The operators are supposed to be screening their calls, but you wouldn't believe how resourceful the American press can be. According to a three-page memo we received this morning, no one working on this show is to speak to journalists of any stripe or description. I think anyone who disobeys will be shot at dawn." Her phone rang. "Back to my post," she said cheerily. "I'm beginning to understand why casting directors love their work. You can get a real rush from rejecting people. Your copy of the memo is on your desk." And she left me alone to peruse it.

It was a standard Lucy/Linda release: a lot of sweet verbiage about the ABN family cloaking some nasty threats. There were hints of unpleasant reprisals for those who broke the faith. Especially if the details of Gregg's floral adornment were leaked. Extra guards would be posted outside the Broadcast Center to keep the press from harassing us. These stalwarts would maintain the same schedule as the police squad, staying on duty until the day's work had ended and the nighttime security system was activated.

The message was, no lingering after school and never talk to strangers. Personally, I didn't think we'd be keeping the details of Gregg-Gate a secret for long no matter what we did.

I threw down the memo and circled the room. Sitting still was out of the question. The unwanted attention from the press was unsettling. But that wasn't the only reason for my restlessness. Too many strange little twists were turning up in the psyches of people I thought I knew well. It was disturbing. But, I realized to my horror, it was also kind of exciting. And fascinating. For the first time in my life I could almost understand those creeps who bring their cameras to a four-car pile-up on the freeway.

Chapter
Eight

I knew Larry would come to the studio because he had scheduled a nine-thirty interview with a new outline writer. Under the circumstances most people would have canceled, but not Larry. He marched down the hallway to the writers' office looking doomed but admirable. I don't know why professionalism blows me away when I find it in other people. I always expect it from myself.

It wouldn't be fair to say that I spent the rest of the morning lying in wait for him. Not all of it. But I did manage to spot him as he passed my door on the way to his appointment with Teresa. I grabbed him and pulled him into my office.

"Why didn't you call Gregg on the phone in the writers' office?" I demanded.

"What? I don't have time for this. I have an appointment with . . ."

"Teresa O'Hanlon in half an hour, I know. That's why I'm asking you to explain to me why, when you were here night before last, you didn't call Gregg's office before you left the building? Why did you wait until you got home? You have a key to the writers' office. There is an in-house phone there. Why didn't you simply pick it up, buzz Gregg's office, and find out if he was still here?"

"I guess I didn't think of it."

"I know you, Larry, it's the first thing you would have thought of—if you were here."

There were so many ways he could have answered. What he said, after a long pause, was, "I guess I'll just count on the fact that Detective O'Hanlon doesn't know me as well as you do."

Before I could tell him what a monumentally dumb statement that was, he left.

He never came back to the studio. I know because I was watching for him. And going slightly nuts with what I kept telling myself was nothing more than idle curiosity. By the end of the day, I stopped kidding myself. I was desperately worried and frantic for information. I was contemplating disguising my voice and calling Larry's home when Nan buzzed me. "Lieutenant O'Hanlon has requested your presence at her office," she said. "What exactly is the difference between a lieutenant and a sergeant?"

"I'm not sure. I think they did an episode of *Cagney and Lacey* about it."

"And very sensitive it was, I'm sure. Would you like the address of the precinct?"

I know there are police stations in New York. I've walked past a couple and I see them regularly on the six o'clock news. I just never expected to go inside one. By the time I reached the entrance of the Twentieth Precinct I was so unnerved I'd almost forgotten about Larry and his plight.

The desk sergeant directed me to Teresa's office

on the second floor. I squeezed onto a crowded elevator hoping fervently that none of my fellow passengers were felons.

The detective division wasn't nearly as big or chaotic as I'd thought it would be from watching *Hill Street Blues*. There were maybe ten desks crammed together in a narrow, gray room with no windows. I had an impression of paperwork piled so high it threatened to take over all empty space, and young guys all talking at once on their phones. One sported a gun in a shoulder holster. Teresa was nowhere in sight. The cop with the gun gave me a smile worthy of a toothpaste commercial, and told me I could wait for Detective O'Hanlon in her office. This proved to be a tiny cubbyhole with glass walls at the far end of the room. I went in as instructed.

A large American flag on a pedestal dominated one entire corner of the office. I wondered if it was something Teresa had brought in from home to spiff up her work space. Her desk was immaculate, of course. There were no bulging accordion files spilling over onto the blotter. A neat stack of manila folders sat in a wire basket on one side of the desk next to her phone, her notepad, and two well-sharpened pencils. On the other side were several photographs. As I moved in for a closer look, I told myself that I wasn't being nosy. The first picture was of a good-looking young man in police uniform who was laughing happily at the camera. Next to it were two photos in a double frame. The subjects were also policemen, both in their early thirties, both striking the same unsmiling pose. The photographs were clearly from another era; the uniform in one looked like a period costume. The third picture was a family portrait. I picked it up. It was an informal outdoor shot, probably taken in the backyard. Mom and Dad were in the center, flanked by three boys with gentle eyes, and a little girl of about five whose firm, no-nonsense expression I already knew well.

"My family," said a voice from behind me. I executed a rather tricky little half pirouette en l'air and found myself facing Teresa O'Hanlon.

"Hi there. I was just . . ." I trailed off. The picture was burning a hole in my hands.

Teresa nodded sympathetically. "Yes. Photographs are always such a temptation, aren't they?" She dodged the flag with practiced grace and came to my side so she could look with me.

"That's Mom and Pop," she said. "And those are my brothers; Sean, Michael, and Patrick."

I studied the picture for a moment, then stared at the double frame. "Isn't this your father, too?" I asked, indicating the newer of the two photos.

"Yes, and the other one is his father."

"Police work seems to run in your family."

"I'm third-generation cop," she said. I could feel her pride. She picked up the pictures of her father and grandfather. "These were taken twenty-five years apart, on the day each of them was promoted to lieutenant. Now I carry their shield."

I didn't follow and it must have showed. "The

numbers on police shields are never retired," she explained. "They're handed down to the next generation of cops. My father asked for his father's shield number and got it. When I made lieutenant, I asked for Pop's shield and they gave it to me." She put the pictures down. "The department has many traditions that the public never knows about."

"What about your brothers? Didn't any one of them want the shield?"

A smile tugged at the side of her mouth. I got a glimpse of Teresa off-duty. And then, "My brothers decided not to walk in their father's footsteps. Sean is staying home to raise his four kids. Michael teaches Romance philology at a small college in Vermont. And Patrick is Mother Maggie."

Except for that first moment, she had a deadpan delivery that was as good as mine. Either that, or she didn't know she was being funny.

"Patrick is who?" I demanded.

"Mother Maggie. It's the name of his bakery. You've probably eaten his apple pie. He sells it to most of the good restaurants in town. It's delicious, he uses four different kinds of apples."

"An old family secret, no doubt."

"Not really. Mom is a terrible cook."

"So you're the only policeman . . . person in the crowd."

"I was always more athletic than the boys."

I looked at the last picture. "And who is the fellow with the terrific smile?" I asked.

The transformation which came over her was

amazing. And yet for the life of me I couldn't have said what changed. It was just that all the crispness seemed to melt.

"That was Bobby O'Hanlon," she said quietly. It took me a few seconds to put it together. Then I snuck a peek at the fourth finger of her left hand. I was pretty sure I hadn't seen a ring. She caught me at it.

"We were married right after I graduated from the Academy," she said. "Bobby was with Narcotics. He was killed three and a half years ago."

"I'm sorry," I said somewhat foolishly. She gave me a little nod.

"Please sit down," she said and waited while I maneuvered myself around the flag.

"Now then," she said pleasantly. "What can you tell me about your Mr. Bradley?"

It wasn't the first time she'd shifted gears on me, going from friendly chat to interrogation, so it shouldn't have thrown me. But it did.

"He's not mine," I blurted. "There's a Mrs. Bradley."

"Yes. Christina." Teresa studied me for a second. I had the feeling she was giving herself a last chance to back out of some decision she'd already made. Instead she plunged in. "About five days ago Christina Bradley wrote a note to Gregg Whithall. It was hand-delivered by her to the doorman at Mr. Whithall's apartment building. However, we found it in Mr. Whithall's desk at the Broadcast Center. In it she cancels a luncheon date which was to have taken place at his apartment and hopes he will understand why she couldn't 'go through with it.' "

I tried not to let my jaw drop. I tried to keep my heart from pounding out loud. Teresa carried on.

"This morning Mr. Bradley told me that two nights ago he was working late at home and discovered that he needed a disc which he had left at the office. That, he claims, is why he went back to the studio after hours."

It was a stupid story, especially for a writer as good as Larry. Especially since his wife seemed to have been a pen pal of the dear departed. But then, Larry was being very stupid—a trait I hated to see in someone I once thought I was going to marry.

"Coincidences do happen," I offered.

"All the time. And it could be nothing more than a coincidence that Mr. Bradley happened to be on the site of a murder at eleven o'clock when our coroner says the crime took place between ten and midnight. But I'd feel a lot better if I thought that Mr. Bradley appreciated the seriousness of his situation. This is not play-acting."

"I'm sure Larry understands that."

"I'm not. Because he is lying to me."

I didn't know how to answer that one. He was lying to me, too.

"I asked you to come here because I was hoping you could help me. Do you know why he's lying?"

I shook my head. I had a couple of theories, but I hated them a lot.

"I told Mr. Bradley about his wife's note. He

seemed genuinely surprised . . ."

She paused so I could comment. I didn't.

". . . however, even after I told him, he stuck to his story. I know you're close to Mr. Bradley, and I'm sure you can understand how bad all of this looks for him."

"I don't know what's going on with Larry. But I can tell you that he didn't kill Gregg. Larry couldn't kill anyone." There was a pleading note in my voice that I couldn't control. Teresa either didn't hear it or chose to ignore it. She stood up.

"I know you want to help Mr. Bradley. So please think about everything I've told you. And if you do have any influence with him, impress upon him the importance of telling us the truth. We'll discover it eventually. We always do."

She wasn't trying to scare me, she was just stating a fact. And she was worried. That was what made me get the hell out of there as fast as I could and race back to my office.

Chapter
Nine

I knew Larry hadn't been in the building on the fateful night. When I'd confronted him with the phone call he hadn't made, he hadn't given me an argument. And if there was an argument, Larry would have made it. So who else could have gotten her little white hands on Larry's ID card? Who could have raided his wallet while he was taking a shower or brushing his teeth because she lived with him? And who could cause Larry, normally a super-bright man, to start behaving like the muscle-bound hero of a mindless action movie?

I waited until I was sure Nan was on the other line, then I called his home. The lady of the house answered, of course, and it took a lot of maturity to hold off my explosion until I got to Larry. Then I went sky-high.

"How dare you?" I screeched. "How dare you allow your testosterone to rot out your brain cells? To go all hairy-chested masculine and stupid when . . ."

"Ange," Larry tried to stem the tide, "not now. Chrissie . . ."

"Cannot be held responsible. She was born with an IQ equal to her shoe size. But you know better. You can't lie to the police, Larry. Christina was the one who went to the studio. To get back her note to Gregg. And you knew nothing about it.

She probably told you she was going to a cupcake-baking class. Now you're trying to protect . . ."

"Ange, does the phrase 'mind your own business' have any resonance for you?"

"You need a lawyer—yesterday. You can't fool around . . ."

"Angela, shut up." He really wanted me to. I could hear it in his voice.

"Sorry," I said. "I must have a wrong number." And I hung up.

I told myself it was a good thing. I told myself that now whatever part of my heart had been hanging on to him would have to let go. I told myself a lot of bullshit. It got me through the rest of the day.

When I left the building the security guards and the police were gone and so was the press. Probably somebody had decapitated someone somewhere. The outside of the Broadcast Center felt deserted. And dark. I found myself walking fast to hail a cab.

However, we made the evening news—local and national. A man who was connected in some capacity with the police department stood behind a podium and answered questions from reporters. The Girls hovered in the background. Lucy had replaced her turban with a pink snood. It was not photogenic. The gist of the man's comments, which were carried by all major channels plus cable, was that the police were on the job and they were going to get to the bottom of this thing.

There was no mention of naked corpses or gold lamé roses. Chalk up one for Lucy and Linda.

I munched on my Weight Watchers pepperoni pizza and thought about that rose. I tried to picture Chrissie bringing it with her when she went to commit murder. Packing it with the gun in her Laura Ashley tote bag. I tried to imagine her pulling the gun on Gregg, forcing him to undress. But first she had to force him to go into Steve's dressing room . . . I sat up straight, little cold prickles at the back of my neck. How did she get into Steve's dressing room without a key? Steve had worked the day before and locked it when he left. Or had he? Maybe he was in a hurry to catch his flight to Cleveland and had left the room unlocked. But the dressing room was locked when Magda opened it and found the body. So how did Chrissie lock it without the key? Didn't that let Chrissie off the hook? It was certainly worth mentioning to Teresa. And to Larry.

Chapter
Ten

By the time I arrived at the studio the next morning I was having second thoughts about mentioning my brilliant theory to Teresa. The police were the professionals, I told myself as two guards stepped forward to help me make my way past the reporters. Surely they'd already thought of the dressing room key. If it was important they were probably investigating it already. If it wasn't, they weren't. In either case the last thing they needed was my help. So I should just butt out.

Except that my DNA isn't programmed for butting out. And I was handed such a golden opportunity to butt in.

"All hell is breaking loose in the costume department," Nan announced as I walked into my office.

"Is it a group action, or solo work?"

"It's Steve Robbe."

When I got down to the wardrobe room our leading man was indeed in the middle of an impressive tantrum directed at Marc.

"My people on the Coast warned me about doing daytime, they told me . . ." He spotted me and turned his attention my way without missing a beat. "Angie, I don't have to take this shit. That pilot I shot may still go to series. CBS has been begging, on their knees . . ."

"Steve sweetheart, calm down, talk to me. You know I want to fix it, sweetheart. But how can I, if you don't tell me?" I've found that in moments of stress it is best to communicate with Steve in the patois of his native land, which is Southern California Agentspeak. Before Steve could answer, Marc cut through the crap.

"Steve is upset because the star dressing room is unavailable. The police say we can't use it."

He smirked a little as he said it. Boo repressed a snicker. And I began to understand. Steve is not a popular fav in the costume department. "And where have you reassigned Steve?"

Marc and Boo looked at each other, "Well, Jeffy Dowers is the only one who isn't doubling up . . ." Marc began.

"Angie, the kid's mother teaches him his lines in there," Steve wailed. "She has a metronome and a baton and this huge stopwatch . . ."

I fixed Marc with a stern look. "For the time being you will clean up the big dressing room we use for the extras and give it to Steve. Find some furniture for him. In fact, have someone take the sofa out of my office."

"Angie, I couldn't . . ."

"Sure you could, Steve. I insist."

"And where will I put the extras?" asked Marc angrily.

"They can dress in the men's room. Screw their union. Is everything okay now, Steve?"

"I hope you don't think I was being difficult."

"Never."

I could have let it go at that. I could have walked out of the wardrobe room and gone back to producing my show. Instead I asked, "Steve, are you sure you locked your dressing room door before you left for Cleveland?"

"Positive. I was especially careful because I knew I was going to be gone for a couple of days."

"Have you ever given the key to anyone else?"

"Not even Brucie. Why?"

"No particular reason." I looked around the room. Magda was sitting at her table in the corner sewing as usual. I went over to her. "Magda, was the dressing room locked when you found the body?"

She didn't look up, naturally. "Was locked," she growled into the skirt she was hemming. Such charm.

Marc and Boo were looking at me strangely. I shrugged. "If the murderer had to have a key to Steve's dressing room, that does eliminate quite a few people, don't you think?"

They continued to stare.

"Guys, don't try to tell me that you aren't fascinated by all this. I'll bet the gossip mill has been working triple time."

When I was back out in the hallway I realized that I had just told the two chief feeders of the gossip mill that their fearless leader was dabbling in a little amateur detective work.

Larry was waiting for me back in my office. He looked like hell, but there was a writers' meeting scheduled. And of course, Larry would have come back from the dead to meet with his writers. He was even early. Somewhere in the cosmos the spirit of a tough-minded nanny who believed that punctuality was the virtue of kings was nodding in approval.

"Ange, I'm sorry about yesterday," he said. "I know you were just trying to help."

"As you said, you don't need me butting into your business."

"As you said, I left the door open for it."

"I never said that."

He smiled at me. "No," he said gently. "But you should have."

I do not have bad taste in men.

He started for the door.

"Larry. Are you okay?"

This time the smile came hard. "I'm not sure."

"For what it's worth, I don't think she did it."

"Did what?"

"Murdered Gregg."

"Oh. No, I know she didn't do that."

But he wasn't so sure about some other things. That letter had hit him hard. He managed one more smile before he left.

* * *

After the show wrapped for the day, I stayed behind in the control booth. Through the large glass window that looked out into the studio, I watched as the stagehands turned off first the stage lights, and then the work lights, leaving one lone red warning light winking in the darkness. The huge air conditioners were revved up to produce the arctic blasts necessary for keeping the cameras cool. The soundstage, which is heavily insulated to ensure silence during taping, was hushed and deserted. In the rest of the studio people were calling out "Good night" to each other and happily packing in the workday. On the loading dock the guys were heaving furniture onto the trucks under the watchful eye of Hank and his squad. But in the control booth I felt sealed off from the rest of the world. Which suddenly started making me nervous. I began gathering up my papers quickly. The hinges on the door of the booth are always kept well greased, which is why I didn't hear Teresa come in.

"Damn! Don't sneak up on me like that. I'm jumpy enough already."

"I'm glad to hear it." Teresa closed the door carefully behind her. "Perhaps you can explain why everyone in this studio seems to think that you are helping with the investigation of this murder. Several people I questioned today actually referred me to you."

I cringed. "All I did was ask a couple of questions . . ."

"So I've heard. About Mr. Robbe's dressing

room and the keys and who might have had them and whether the room was locked at the time of the murder. Have I covered everything?"

I nodded.

"I assume you undertook this inquiry in the hopes of exonerating Mr. Bradley and his wife."

"I never said a word about them to anyone."

"You didn't have to. Almost everyone seems to know that Mr. Bradley's ID card was used by someone to get into this building on the night of the murder. And of course everyone knows of your past relationship with Mr. Bradley."

"One thing you can say about *Bright Tomorrow,* our grapevine is the best in the business." I actually felt a swelling of pride.

Teresa was not impressed. "All this careless talk is dangerous. What if the killer were to hear a rumor that you were close to solving the case? Or that you had solved it? Do you understand what kind of response that could trigger?"

I hadn't thought about that, nor did I want to. "No one would believe that I could solve a murder. That would be crazy."

"Are you suggesting that someone who commits murder is sane?"

I shivered involuntarily. "Warning taken."

"Good," said Teresa. But I'm not sure she believed me.

We turned to leave. Then we both stopped short. I'd thought the air in the control booth had been getting colder; now I knew why.

"I know I closed that door," said Teresa in a

voice that was a little too steady. The door was swinging wide open.

Teresa did a thorough search of the soundstage but she didn't find anyone; I had a nasty moment when she pulled out her gun, but after about two minutes I started breathing regularly again and I was fine.

When Teresa questioned the stragglers who were still in the building, no one had seen anyone going into the soundstage after she went in. No one could remember seeing anyone who looked suspicious lurking in the hallway.

As I walked out of the building and into the blessed fresh air, I felt lucky. And stupid. No more playing detective, I told myself. Never again.

Chapter
Eleven

Never say never. At about three o'clock the next afternoon, Marc showed up in my office, looking pale under his salon tan.

"Angie, I can't find my key for Steve Robbe's dressing room," he gasped. "I used to have one key for all the dressing rooms but then Steve was afraid that someone would steal that hideous makeup case. So he had a new lock put on his door and he gave me the key and told me to get it copied for my 'staff' as if he was Princess Di or something. And I had copies made for Boo and Magda and me, although it's all such bullshit because, trust me, no one would be desperate enough to steal that thing . . ."

"Marc . . ."

". . . and anyway now it's gone. My key, not his case. Which is a pity because at least that would prove that there is a God and She has taste. But I . . ."

"Marc!" It's not easy to stop Marc when he's on a roll. But something in my tone must have caught his attention.

"Have you told Detective O'Hanlon?"

"No way. I came straight to you."

I buzzed Nan. "Please find Detective O'Hanlon and tell her to come to my office right away."

"Angie, don't," Marc wailed. "You said yourself that whoever killed Gregg had to have that key. Well, anyone on our show could have taken mine. You know what our wardrobe room is like. Everybody hangs out there. It's like Grand Central Station. If you tell the cops, you'll just make it easier for them to pin it on one of us. They're already trying to do it. Probably because we're in show business and they hate us . . ."

"Marc . . ."

". . . because they all live in Queens and their tacky wives wear polyester and . . ."

"Marc, I am going to have to hurt you. . . ."

"Promise?"

I glared at him.

"Okay, okay. I'll be good."

"When was your key stolen?"

"I don't know."

I told myself that I would gain nothing by braining him with the trophy from *Family Feud*.

"When did you first notice it was missing?"

"This afternoon. But that was only because I went looking for it which I never would have done if you hadn't been asking all those questions. It could have disappeared three months ago for all I know. Or yesterday."

"How could you not notice that one of your dressing room keys is missing?"

"Because I never use them. I don't go to the dressing rooms. That's the scut work. I make Magda and Boo do it. Half the time I don't even know where my keys are. I just drop them wherever. I'm a creative person, I don't do details."

I didn't even let myself glance at the *Family Feud* trophy.

"Marc," I said patiently, "try to follow me. You have to talk to the police. Because before long they will be asking you about your keys and then . . ."

"They already have. Day before yesterday, at ten o'clock in the morning, if you can believe the timing. You know how nuts my wardrobe room is at ten in the morning on a normal day, and that day with everyone crazed about Gregg and getting back to work after we'd been off, it was a complete zoo. And that's when the gestapo chose to descend. So I got them off my back."

"By lying to them?"

"I told them I had all my keys because I thought I did. Somewhere. I mean, Jesus Christ, who knew?"

"You should have."

"Angie, give me a break. My shipment from Saks had just arrived. I was up to my tits in peau de soie and actors."

My hand was itching to grab the *Family Feud* trophy. Fortunately, at that moment Nan wandered in. "Detective O'Hanlon is not in the building. Her minions do not know where she is. Hank wants to know if you'd like him to come up."

Before I could answer, Marc said quickly, "Angie, there's something else you should know. It isn't just the cast and crew who have been in the wardrobe room. Two weeks ago Magda did some alterations for Larry's wife, Chrissie."

I turned to Nan. "Tell Hank it's not necessary," I said.

She shot me a look. Then she turned and walked out.

Marc gave me a peck on the cheek. "I knew you'd make the right decision," he said happily, and headed for the door.

"If you didn't want the cops to know about this, why the hell didn't you keep it to yourself?"

He looked at me in amazement.

"But then I might be withholding information from the police. This way it's your decision."

I almost picked up the trophy. I actually reached for it.

"You are the boss, Angie," he went on, blissfully unaware of the danger he was in. "You always tell us to bring the big problems to you. Besides, I thought it might be a clue you needed. To help you solve the murder."

"I am not solving . . ." I began, but stopped because he had closed the door on his way out.

What I had just done shook me. I didn't know how serious it would be if I didn't tell the police what I knew, but I did know I'd be breaking the law. My family may be eccentric, but with the exception of Uncle Paulie we've always been law-abiding to the point of boredom. It's probably a reaction to all those movies about colorful Italian mobsters eating pasta with machine guns strapped over their undershirts. I could just see my mother's face if I wound up in jail. Even worse, I could hear her.

But then as I sat in my comfortable armchair something else started kicking in: the old slightly sick, slightly mesmerized accident-on-the-freeway excitement. And a lot of curiosity.

I moved to the phone and dialed Larry's home number. At some point Teresa was going to hunt me down to find out what I'd wanted to say. I wasn't sure how honest I planned to be, but I did know that before I went any farther out on a limb I wanted some answers.

To my amazement, it was Larry, not Chrissie, who picked up the phone. On a writing day. Even more amazing, he agreed to come to my office immediately. On a writing day.

He got to the studio in twenty minutes. It took another ten for him to get past security and come upstairs to my office.

"Where's Chrissie?" I asked as soon as I had closed my office door.

"She's gone away for a few days. To visit a friend."

"That letter of hers really rocked you, didn't it?"

It was the wrong thing to say. Especially for me. The temperature in the room dropped many degrees as he stiffened his upper lip to the rigidity appropriate for a Bradley fielding inappropriate questions.

"What did you want to talk about, Ange?" he asked coolly.

"Chrissie. And Gregg. And were they getting it on?" When Larry gets on his high horse I always take the low road.

"I hardly think . . ."

"Cut the old school tie crap, Larry. I'm not prying into your personal life so I can dish your wife when I lunch at the Yale Club. God knows why, but I want to help you. If I can. And since you're in no position to turn down help from any source, you'd better level with me. Besides, it would do you good to talk."

Sometimes when you least expect him to, a man will listen to reason. Larry seemed to flatten into my armchair. Like a rubber ball losing air. I wondered how long it had been since he'd had a good night's sleep.

"Okay, Ange," he said in a voice of defeat. "I'll tell you all of it."

I promised myself I wouldn't open my mouth until he finished talking. If it killed me.

He began wearily. "Chrissie says that she flirted with Gregg just one time. At your welcome-back party. Because she was so jealous of you."

She was jealous?

"She's always felt that I married her on the rebound. And that night she was upset because you and I spent so much time together."

Discussing the budget for his new storyline. I've had sexier conversations with my periodontist.

"Chrissie flirted with Gregg to get my attention. She thought it was harmless. But Gregg . . . well, you know what an egomaniac he was when it came to women. Even after he started losing all his hair he still thought he was God's gift."

And they say women are catty.

"Gregg started coming on to Chrissie. She panicked because he was my boss and she didn't want to insult him, so she finally agreed to have lunch with him. Gregg told her . . . Ange, I can't stand it anymore."

"Stand what?"

"You've had at least three good openings to zing me. If you keep holding back like this you're going to hurt yourself."

"Are you saying that I can't be sensitive?"

"I'm saying you're going to rupture something if you keep going against nature."

"I believe you had gotten as far as Chrissie's lunch with Gregg," I said primly.

He got back on track fast.

"The bastard was such a manipulator. He didn't make a move toward her, of course. He just talked about the show. Then he got on to you and I and what a great team we had been. And still were. He told her about Claire Wingate. That he wanted to bring the character back, but you were fighting him and I was going to back you."

I didn't know that.

"He made it sound as if I was doing it because I hadn't backed you the last time and now I wanted to make it up with you."

What a sweetheart. He was going to back me.

"He said we'd broken up the first time because we were fighting over Claire Wingate. He suggested that I regretted it. He played on all Chrissie's insecurities."

With those legs she's insecure?

"Chrissie's not gullible exactly. But she's not . . ."

Operating on all thrusters? Of this planet?

". . . tough."

Ah.

"She let herself be talked into seeing him again."

You betcha.

"This time lunch was going to be at his apartment."

Natch.

"When she got home she realized what she'd done. She wanted to cancel their lunch. She couldn't call him because she didn't want to leave a message at the studio during the day and I'm usually at home at night."

So she put it in writing. Clever girl.

"So she wrote that note. Gregg was furious. He threatened to show it to me. She begged him to give it back. Finally he set up the meeting at the studio so they could talk. But when she got there he didn't show. So she came home. I wanted to know where she'd been. She told me Gregg was harassing her and she'd gone to the studio to put a stop to it. She was afraid to tell me about the lunch and the note."

He got up and prowled around the room. "I want to believe her."

The next words out of my mouth surprised both of us.

"I do," I said.

Because that story is so stupid it's got to be true, I didn't say.

The effect of the statement on Larry was spectacular. First he turned red, then his eyes started to fill. I was terrified that he was going to do something horrible like cry. I'd never seen Larry lose it. When we were together I used to complain about his iron control. Now that he was falling apart in front of me, I wanted to be in another neighborhood.

It occurred to me that I could take away a lot of his stress by telling him about Marc's missing key. If it had been stolen, that could broaden the field of suspects considerably. But Larry would insist on telling the police. And I still had some major ruminating to do on that one.

"One thing does interest me about your beloved," I said. "Why the hell is she willing to let you take the rap for her? Why hasn't she told the police she was in the building on the night of the murder?"

"I would imagine that was Mr. Bradley's idea," said a familiar voice behind me. Larry and I both whirled around to see Teresa standing in the doorway. She and Larry exchanged a look.

"Chrissie told you," he said.

Teresa nodded. "She came to the police station this morning to give us her statement."

"She wanted to from the very beginning," he

said. "I wouldn't let her. I . . ." He stopped to get a grip on himself again.

"Yes. I had the feeling Mrs. Bradley was very relieved to be talking to us," said Teresa. Then she turned to me. "I understand you wanted to see me? I got here as quickly as I could but I'm afraid I don't have much time."

Without meaning to, I looked toward Larry. It was the expression in his eyes that did it. I decided what I wanted to do about the police and Marc's key. And I wanted Larry out of the room while I did it. I looked at him again and hesitated.

Teresa picked up on it. "Perhaps it would be better if we spoke privately?" she said.

"Of course." Larry headed for the door, happy to have the opportunity to pull himself together alone. Teresa marched into the office and positioned herself in the middle of the rug. My rug. In my office. In my studio.

"Now what did you want to tell me?" she asked.

"It's nothing important," I said.

She frowned ever so slightly. "I understood from Hank that it was urgent," she said carefully.

"Well, it is and it isn't," I improvised, stalling for time. "I mean it's important to me, but not important enough for you to come racing over here."

Teresa stared at me.

"My problem is . . ." I searched my brain frantically for a problem and found one. A real one, as it happened. "The problem is, I've got a group of schoolkids coming to tour my studio next week. I was wondering if they'll need passes of some kind to show your security guards?"

Teresa's frown deepened. "Are you sure that's all?"

"It may not seem like much to you, but I don't want thirty-eight kids plus mothers from P.S. 72 milling around the lobby. Some of those mothers are community activists and they can get militant."

I never would have gotten away with it if Teresa hadn't been in such a rush. She didn't believe me, but she just didn't have the time to do anything about it.

"I'll see to your passes," she said as she moved toward the door. "And perhaps the next time we talk you will remember why you wanted to speak to me. The real reason."

She looked closer than I'd ever seen her to losing her temper as she closed the door a bit too firmly behind her.

That night I dreamed a variation on my standard anxiety nightmare. It featured a gold lamé rose that seemed to be growing out of my navel and someone whose face I could not see who was connected with *Bright Tomorrow* in some way I couldn't remember. And Mama wasn't singing the "Italian Street Song." She was humming the theme from *The Godfather*.

Chapter
Twelve

The next morning in the cab on my way to work I entertained myself by conjuring up several possible hair-raising scenarios in which Teresa hauled me down to the police station for questioning. And when I refused to crack, incarceration. I fantasized some Barbara Stanwyck moments of dignity for myself and then had a panic attack because the only lawyer I know is a guy in my building who used to work in real estate before the bottom fell out of the Manhattan market.

By the time I got to my office I was expecting to see Teresa camped out in front of it with hoses and dogs. But she was nowhere around. And no one had seen her. And the front lobby guards weren't expecting her.

At first I was relieved, then I figured maybe it was a ploy, that she was giving me time to brood so I'd be softened when she went in for the kill. Then I told myself I was being crazy. Which I was, but I cut myself some slack because, after all, I'd never been a criminal before.

I got enlightenment on Teresa's whereabouts when I met Vinnie on the bagel line. "The detective's outta town for a coupla days. Could be our case, could be something else she's working on. She don't just work on one thing at a time." He had this information from his new best friend, Hank.

Feeling far more relaxed, I wandered around the soundstage looking for Nate. Several people had seen him, but I couldn't find him. Which could or could not have meant that he was dodging me. Tommy Props wasn't anywhere in sight.

Back upstairs in my office I wrote a memo to Nate asking him to be sure he saw me before the day ended. I thought of writing one to Anna, but a quick check of the schedule told me she wasn't working until the next day. Besides, I wasn't quite sure how to approach the question I wanted to ask Anna. "Isn't it weird for you to be weeping for a man you loathed?" didn't quite seem tactful. Especially since there were many who would have said that weird was a natural state for Anna Martin.

After a little more thought, I walked down the hall to the in-house mailboxes and delivered my message myself. No point in making Nan any more curious than she already was.

After that there didn't seem to be anything more I could do. Except the job for which I was being paid. So I got to it, forcing myself to concentrate on the scripts for the next week's shows instead of gold lamé roses.

I was just blacking out a reference to the Dark Lady of the Sonnets—Larry hires classy dialogue writers who periodically forget our audience—when Nan came in.

"A treat is in store for you," she announced. "The Girls wish to take you to lunch. Lucy Stone's secretary is on the phone even as we speak."

"Make her go away."

"I gather her boss is in a froth."

"Lucy's always in a froth. It's how she keeps her metabolism up."

"This time, O Captain, my Captain, she has cause."

"Says she."

Nan sighed. "I was afraid you hadn't seen it." She handed me one of those loathsome supermarket tabloids, adding, "Thank God one of us has a taste for sleazy journalism."

I wasn't surprised that the full story had finally blown sky-high. After all, the press already had the laundered version of it. It was a miracle that we'd been able to keep the juicy stuff out of the papers for as long as we had. But somehow I wasn't prepared to see the whole mess in print.

Gregg had made the front page. Not the big center spread. That was given over to a member of the British royal family who had been caught nuzzling a married woman who looked like his polo pony and the latest story on Oprah Winfrey's love life. Gregg rated a small picture in the upper right-hand corner. It was a smiling head shot, at least ten years old, reproduced in garish Technicolor. However, they did spell his name right. And they were very clear about the fact that he'd been killed in the *Bright Tomorrow* studio.

The story on the inside pages was illustrated with black-and-white shots of a naked corpse which could have been Gregg, but were too blurry for me to be certain. Black blocks had been coyly printed over strategic areas of the body for modesty's sake, so there was no picture of the blossom and bows. The accompanying story was full of ugly innuendo and partial truths, dwelling on the kinkiness of the crime and the fact that the corpse was found in our leading man's dressing room. Reference was made to an artificial flower and the organ to which it had been attached. However, it was never specified that the flower was a gold lamé rose. Sources close to Daytime Vice President Lucy Stone were quoted throughout; no mention was made of Daytime Vice President Linda McCain. I tossed the paper. No way around it, the sly suggestions about the probable sexual proclivities of members of our cast could hurt us. But the real problem was, the story was funny. And ABN Daytime was the butt of the joke. That had to be driving them wild out in L.A.

"Tell The Girls we're on for lunch," I said unhappily.

"I already have. Lucy has made reservations for one o'clock at California Dreamin'."

I sighed. "Of course she has." From the day it opened, I've hated California Dreamin'.

Nan turned to go. Then she turned back.

"By the way, I'm still available to take your memos down to the mailbox," she said. Before I could answer she was gone.

Chapter Thirteen

The Upper West Side used to be loaded with great ethnic restaurants. The waiters in these establishments did not want to be actors when they grew up, the cooks were not chefs, and the plastic-covered booths did not create an "ambience." But the food was fabulous. You could eat your way up Broadway from 72nd to 110th Street and never taste the same cuisine twice.

Then we got invaded by the fern bars. Now you can take your pick of identical hot spots with bare brick walls and the review from *New York* magazine displayed prominently in the floor-to-ceiling front window.

The worst of these eateries, for my money, is California Dreamin'. It's the kind of place you could find in any suburban shopping mall, except that the water comes to you direct from Italy in little green bottles and the low-fat burgers cost $22.85 because the animals from which they came never touched foot to ground during their lifetime. It was the perfect place for lunch with The Girls.

Or perhaps only one Girl. Lucy was alone when she met me at the entrance to the restaurant, an unusual occurrence because she usually likes to be seated before her lunch companions arrive. I think it's a power thing.

"I don't know where Linda is," she fretted as

we were led to our table. "I've been calling her office all morning. I don't like this one little bit. It's . . . Oh my God, it's Michael."

I turned in the direction she was indicating to see the president of ABN, Michael Libson, seated at a banquette.

"What's he doing here?" I asked. "Doesn't he turn into a pillar of salt if he leaves Los Angeles for longer than four hours?"

But Lucy wasn't laughing. "I should have known," she said grimly. "That bitch." Whereupon she stretched her lips into the smile she considers winning and headed for Michael.

Who did not greet her warmly, it seemed to me. But then Michael Libson never seems warm to me—or even human. It's become fashionable among the young actresses he constantly propositions to describe him as sexy, but I don't think anyone really means it. He has a great body thanks to a trainer—who, it is rumored, accompanies him even on romantic trysts—and a taste for restaurants like California Dreamin'. He sports designer hair and suits, but beautiful he isn't. It's his eyes mostly. They're cold, pale blue, and a little too big for their sockets. His mouth is wide and his nose is flat. The overall effect is that of a frog decked out in Armani. I never see Michael Libson without wanting to offer him a few dead flies. For a variety of reasons.

Now he was looking at Lucy with revulsion, as if she'd just suggested that he do something filthy like eat dessert. He held her at arm's length for their ritual air kiss which caused her to babble nervously.

"Michael, darling, why didn't you tell me . . . it's too lovely of course, but I wasn't expecting . . . How long are you staying?"

"Until Linda and I can straighten out this mess with the tabloids. I've had several calls from sponsors already. They're all terrified of those Christian boycott groups. This is not the kind of publicity we want in this day and age, Lucy."

"I know. And of course I'll do anything . . ."

"You've done quite enough—since the leak came from your staff in the first place."

"My staff? My staff?" Lucy started with a squeak and built to a screech. Several people turned to look. Four of them recognized Michael and waved frantically. He turned a nasty shade of purple which made him look like a frog in the throes of apoplexy.

Lucy recognized her error at once. She forced another grin and slipped into the banquette next to him.

"Michael dear, I think it's fabulous that you want to be involved in fixing this—it's such a dynamic leadership move, and so *you*. But have you thought at all about the murder itself?"

Michael looked baffled. I couldn't figure where she was heading either.

"It's the timing I wonder about. I mean there was Gregg, ready to fire Linda . . ."

"What?" Michael and I spoke in unison.

"Oh yes." Lucy purred. "He really couldn't

stand having her around. It was the way she looked, poor thing." She patted Michael's perfectly defined bicep. "Dear Gregg was positively phobic about fat people." She slid out of the banquette triumphantly as in the doorway the hostess was showing Linda where Michael was seated.

"Come, Angie," said Lucy. And led me to our table.

"Lucy," I said after we'd ordered. "Are you sure . . . ?"

"About Gregg and Linda? Dearie, when it was just the three of us, he was awful to her. Said the most humiliating things. It was supposed to be teasing and good fun but I tell you it would have driven me to murder." She looked at her fancy water and frowned. "I need a drink," she announced.

When I got back to my office, Nate Bernstein was waiting for me.

"You wanted to see me?" he asked. It seemed to me that he was more than a little belligerent. But then maybe I was edgy because I was about to try my first interrogation. And I had just realized that I didn't know how to interrogate. At least not on purpose.

"Uh," I began nervously, "it's about that gold lamé rose . . ."

"Have they figured out where it came from?" he asked too quickly.

"I don't know. In fact I was going to ask you . . ."

"How about the age? Do they know how old it was?"

It occurred to me that I was losing control of the situation.

"Why?" I said with all the authority I could muster. "Is it important? What do you know about the rose, Nate?"

For a moment I thought he just might tell me. Instead he said, "Oh, fuck it," and walked out.

That night I dreamed about gold lamé roses again. No Mama, no bathtub. Just the roses and the faceless person who was connected to *Bright Tomorrow,* but I didn't know how. Also I think I did a lot of running around because I woke up feeling tired.

As I lay in bed trying to focus, I looked up at my canopy, which had been recycled from a soap opera fantasy sequence. We don't do many fantasies on Daytime these days. But there was a time when they were all the rage. Some of the more spectacular ones had made soap opera history. Suddenly I sat up, blown away by the fact that I'd just had a brainstorm and it was long before noon.

Chapter
Fourteen

There are many ways to research the back stories of a long-running soap. The networks all maintain archives and most of the fan magazines have libraries of back issues. Believe it or not, there are also two or three scholarly tomes on the subject in the Lincoln Center Library for the Performing Arts. But my source is a lot more fun.

"It's the DaVito. Oh joy. Oh rapture." Raymond St. Clair's big fruity baritone boomed at me over the phone. "How may I serve my Queen?"

"I need some information, Ray."

"How wonderful. Does it have to do with your murder? I only know what I read but it sounds like the perfect end for that male bimbo. Dear Jesse, her taste in men was always appalling. You come to me for dinner this evening and give me the real dirt. May I order something luscious from the local charcuterie or must I defrost one of those ghastly diet meals in plastic for you?"

It was almost eight o'clock by the time I managed to present myself at his loft in lower Manhattan. Ray greeted me with open arms. He hadn't changed much since his glory days as Jesse's leading man on *Bright Tomorrow*. There had been a couple of discreet face-lifts and his glossy curls were a skillfully reproduced shade of chestnut.

However, the hair was his own. No plugs or tou-pees for Ray. He was fleshier than he had been when he was the heartthrob of housewives across America, but he could still carry off the velvet smoking jacket he'd chosen to wear for our dinner.

Ray's last year on *Bright Tomorrow* was my first. He'd chosen to retire, saying to me, "I'm not quite the beauty I once was, dear heart. Soon they'll be asking me to act and I've never had the gift."

What he did have, in addition to style and looks, was a business head. During his peak earning years he bought up real estate in neighborhoods no one else would touch. When gentrification hit Manhattan, Ray held three blocks of town houses on the Upper West Side and several old factory buildings in what was soon to be SoHo. He had already converted them into glitzy lofts.

After he finished hugging me he stood back and frowned. "Angela, we must buy you some of these new short skirts immediately. God did not give you those gams so you could hide them under that schmattah."

I've never been wild about my legs but at that moment I felt like heavy competition for Miss America. Ray has that effect on most women.

He led me into his loft, settled me into one of his overstuffed couches, and went off to his kitchen area to microwave my Lean Cuisine while I let my eyes adjust to the murky pink glow which bathes his home. The first time I visited Ray I thought I was having eye problems until I realized that all his lighting comes from overhead kliegs, indirectly focused and covered with gels of Du-Barry Pink, the shade favored by Hollywood stars of a certain age. One subdued spotlight is trained on the throne-like chair in which Ray always sits. Another spot casts a gentle beam on the shelves of white leather-bound scrapbooks which fill one complete wall of the living area. These scrapbooks contain all the letters, fan magazine articles, pictures, and other memorabilia Ray collected during his career as a t.v. idol. Volumes fifteen through twenty-two chronicle his years on *Bright Tomorrow*.

"Perhaps you should tell Father what it is you want to know before you attack my vanity wall physically," said Ray after I had finished my Lean Cuisine zucchini lasagna.

"Do you remember a fantasy sequence on *Bright Tomorrow*—it was before my time but I think it was a wedding—in which everything was gold?"

"The Golden Wet Dream we nicknamed it. You do have a taste for ancient history. I doubt anyone remembers it now, but at the time it made quite a sensation. Of course it was really nothing more than a publicity stunt. *Bright Tomorrow* was the first ABN daytime show to broadcast in color and the network wanted to do something spectacular as a kickoff. Jesse and I were a hot romance at that time, we'd been playing unrequited love and sexual frustration for eighteen months. So they married us off in a big wedding, then did some-

thing which I can't remember to keep us from con-
summating our lust, and let Jesse, or rather Claire,
have a dream in which the same wedding was reproduced in gold. They sprayed the set with gold
paint, reworked the props, and the costumes were
redone in gold fabric.

"Jesse actually looked rather smashing in her
getup. You can imagine all that white-gold hair
under a gold lace veil and yards of gold silk bil-
lowing out from that tiny little waist. I didn't fare
so well, I'm afraid. I don't care how well you wear
it, in a gold lamé tux you will always look like
you sing behind the showgirls in a second-string
Vegas lounge. But the Golden Wet Dream was the
beginning of big popularity for both of us."

"Do you have a picture of that wedding?"

"Of course. It was in all the fan mags back
then." He went straight to volume seventeen, and
opened it to the correct section as if he had the
thing memorized. I didn't like to think about the
long solitary hours he must have spent rereading
those scrapbooks under his pink lights.

I found what I was looking for in a full-page
color picture of Jesse which had graced the cover
of some magazine long gone. Ray was right. Even
in that badly reprinted old picture she was beautiful, a fragile creature with huge, violet-blue eyes
floating in clouds of gold fabric. And in her hands
was a bouquet of one dozen long-stemmed roses.
Made out of gold lamé. I held my breath.

"Ray, do you know what happened to those
roses after the show?"

"Lord love you, child, that was a million years ago."

"Please try to think. It's very important."

He studied me for a second. "You think there's a connection, don't you?"

"I don't know what you're talking about," I said, but Ray was much too smart to be derailed.

"You think one of those roses might be the mysterious flower I've been reading about in the tabloids. The one that was attached to the now defunct Whithall love muscle."

I nodded.

"How thrilling." He shuddered happily and began to concentrate. "Let me see . . . Now that you mention it, it seems to me that people took all kinds of things from that set. None of it could ever have been used again, and, as I said, that show was considered historic. I suppose anyone could have pinched a posy or two for a souvenir." He looked at my face. "That was not what you wanted to hear."

"It's not very specific."

"Yes. It would be more helpful if I could come up with a name. I see that."

He looked so dejected that I felt terrible. "It's okay, Ray . . ." I began. He silenced me with a majestic wave of his hand.

"Wait," he intoned. "I do remember that in the script the bridal bouquet was caught by the youngest bridesmaid, if that's any help. Now what was the character's name? No, it's gone. The part was played by little Anna Martin."

"Anna? She was on the show back then?"

"Didn't you know? She was with us for several years when she was a kid. She was a lovely little actress, reminiscent of the young Julie Harris."

"She never talks about it. I knew her character had been a part of the story in the early days but I didn't know Anna had played the role."

"Ah well, that was back before her troubles, poor baby. Perhaps she doesn't want to remind people. Personally, I always thought those managers of hers should have been hanged. They put so much pressure on the child and anyone could see that she was very highly strung . . ."

"Ray . . ."

". . . and the mother was no help at all. A simple woman, completely dazzled by the money . . . You spoke, my Queen?"

"I hate to interrupt your flow, but what 'troubles' did Anna have?"

"She had a breakdown, darling. At fourteen. Went home from work one night after the show and started crying and couldn't stop. Exhaustion was what those vultures who managed her called it, but there were rumors of electroshock treatments. They were trying to get her back in harness as quickly as possible. It was all very *Snake Pit* if you can remember that perfectly ghastly movie."

"When did this happen?"

"Now that you mention it I think it was right after the Golden Wet Dream. It was a tense time for all of us because the network had so much riding on that show. I guess poor little Anna just snapped. Then it took several years for her to get well again in spite of all the fancy electronics. After which it took even longer for her to reestablish herself because she'd been out of the game for so long. And just between us chickens, she never really did regain all the ground she'd lost. People had been predicting big things for that child, but you know how this business is. That was why she was so glad to return to *Bright Tomorrow* when they decided to bring back her character as a grown woman. The pickings had been mighty slim for her."

"I can't believe *Bright Tomorrow* was willing to gamble on her," I said.

"Well, darling, they were and they weren't." The look on my face must have told him that I wasn't up for riddles because he hurried on. "For the first year she had to work without a contract. To prove herself. Which I always thought was downright evil, but then of course no one ever asked me. However I suppose all's well that et cetera, because she's been back for at least fifteen years and one understands she's fine now."

She was until Gregg was murdered, I thought. "She's swell," I said.

"I'm glad. She always was a sweet kid. A little Looney Tunes about animals, but given the humans in her life, who could blame her? Will you have a postprandial liqueur? I have some anisette that will knock your socks off."

*   *   *

Ray once told me that when he was choosing his own personal residence from among his many holdings, a quiet neighborhood was his main prerequisite. That was why he finally chose to live in a building which was located in an unquaint section of the old meat-packing district. It was a part of town, he assured me, which would never appeal to the restaurant and gallery crowd.

And his incredible instinct for real estate had not failed him. During the day his narrow cobblestoned street was heavily used by the trucks bringing deliveries in from the nearby docks. But when I left Ray at eleven o'clock everything had shut down and the area was as peaceful as the tomb. And as dark and deserted. As I stepped onto the sidewalk in front of his building, a sharp cold wind blew in from the Hudson. A hairy creature with teeth scurried out of a hole in the gutter and I remembered that Ray had once mentioned something about a problem with rats. Needless to say, there wasn't a cab in sight.

I began walking, suddenly aware that my back was too exposed. To what I couldn't have said, but little shivers of fear started running up my spine. No one had followed me, I told myself firmly, even the thought was ridiculous. Something, hopefully a piece of paper caught up by the wind, scuffled at my feet. I didn't look down to see. I picked up my pace, telling myself that I must not run, must not look scared. In case anyone did happen to be following me. Which of course no one was.

A vision of Gregg's face, blue-white on the dressing room table, flashed unbidden in my mind. I started to run. I told myself that those were not footsteps I heard behind me, that the moving shadow on the building walls was my own. I stumbled but I kept going. The cold air was burning my lungs and I was starting to gasp. I promised myself that if I lived I was going to take up jogging—or, at least every once in a while, I'd walk to work.

Then the neighborhood changed as New York City neighborhoods so often do. All of a sudden, there were lights and noise and people and cars—including the most beautiful yellow cab I'd ever seen in my life. I hailed it frantically, threw myself in the back seat, and gasped out my address.

Then I realized that there were tears running down my face.

Chapter
Fifteen

I took a hot bath for hours before I could finally tumble into a dreamless sleep.

Dreamless until morning. When I heard someone pounding on my front door and Larry calling my name. Which had to be a dream. Because there was no way Larry was pounding on my door. Especially not at—I squinted at my bedside clock—six in the morning. But the knocking continued. Until I staggered to the door and opened it. To see Larry standing in front of me holding two cups of coffee in cardboard cups.

"What the hell are you up to, Ange?" he asked at exactly the same moment that I asked, "How did you get in the building?"

"Your doorman," said Larry. "He remembers me. Actually he remembers the scotch I used to give him at Christmas. Answer my question."

"What was it?"

"What game are you up to? I tried to call you all last night."

"I was out."

"Obviously. Where?"

"That's none of your business."

"When you're withholding information from the police because you think you're helping me it becomes my business."

"Who says I'm withholding information from the police?"

"Never mind. Just stop it, Ange."

"You've been talking to Nan, haven't you?"

"That's beside the point. What you're doing is stupid and . . ."

"She had no right to go tattling to you."

"She's worried about you, okay?"

"She doesn't know what I'm doing. Neither do you."

"You said you were going to help me."

"Well, I'm not."

"Good."

Then he leaned over and kissed me. Larry always has to lean over me when he kisses me. It gives me this enclosed feeling, like he's all around me. His whole body. I pressed myself into him and he held me tighter and it felt the way it always had. As if we'd never stopped being together. As if there was no one named Chrissie . . .

The lid on one of the cups must have loosened because hot coffee slopped over his hand and onto the back of my robe. Which didn't matter even a little bit, except that it broke the spell for him. He pulled away abruptly.

"I'm sorry," he said.

"It's only coffee, I'll wash it out."

"You know what I meant."

"Yes, and I'm not sorry."

I was afraid he might leave, but he walked over to the table and put the cups down very carefully. Then he turned and came back, stopping about a yard away from me. I didn't move.

"I don't want you hurting yourself, Ange. Especially not for me. Please."

"I'm not going to get hurt because I'm not doing anything. Just poking around a little. And I'm not doing it for you. Not anymore."

"Then why are you?"

"Because I'm curious. It's like putting together a puzzle, only you have to find the pieces first. Besides, it happened in my studio."

"And one of your friends did it. How are you going to feel if you do trip up and discover which one?"

It was the question I didn't even want to think about. I moved to the table and sat in my usual seat. The one facing away from the window so I don't have to have the sun glaring in my eyes while I try to wake up. I picked up one of the cups of coffee and sipped it. It was still warm.

"Good coffee," I said.

"I thought you'd like it. The guy had to chip it out of the pot with a sharp instrument."

"Where'd you get it?"

"That fancy new market on the corner where the deli used to be. The neighborhood has changed."

"Not necessarily for the better."

"Don't be an old fogey."

He watched me for a second. Then he came over and sat in his old seat across from me.

"What you're doing is dangerous," he said.

"Wasn't that my line to you?"

"Ange."

"Okay. I've been told a few things that O'Hanlon should know. She's been out of town, but she should be back soon. And I am going to tell her everything."

It wasn't a lie. I never said I was going to tell her immediately, or even the next time I saw her. In fact, I was very careful not to say anything like that.

"And you'll stop digging around?" Larry asked sternly.

It was tougher to stay honest on that one.

"Larry, I can't even think where I'd begin to 'dig.'"

Which was true at that moment. I hadn't been awake long enough.

He gave me a big smile as he picked up the other coffee.

We sipped in silence. An uncomfortable silence for me. I wanted to ask him something but I felt shy about it. I hate it when I get hit with these mid-Victorian moments. Finally I came out with it.

"Were you really going to back me on Claire Wingate?"

"Yes."

"Why this time when you wouldn't before?"

"Because this time you were right. Bringing back Claire would have hurt the show. Gregg wanted to do it for his own ego. To prove that he could re-create the character without the actress. It was a personal thing."

"And when he fired Jesse, that wasn't personal?"

"Do we have to rake up ancient history?"

I wished I were the kind of woman who could have let it go. But I wasn't.

"I want to know what's different now."

He sighed. "Firing Jesse was necessary. I believed that. I still do. She'd become a troublemaker; she was trying to polarize the cast, refusing to play storylines, spreading gossip and rumors. If anyone but Jesse had been pulling that crap you'd have been screaming to fire her yourself."

"Larry, the woman was in pain. She'd been used, humiliated . . ."

"She brought it on herself."

"That's not fair."

"Sure it is. Everyone tried to warn her about Gregg. I heard you on the phone for hours begging her not to trust the bastard. But she was the great Jesse Southland. She didn't have to listen to anybody. She had all the answers."

"She fell in love. She made a mistake."

"And you can't blame anyone for that, God knows. But Jesse couldn't take her lumps and admit she'd been a fool. She had to have revenge. And if she destroyed the whole show while she got it, so be it."

"I owed her. And I needed you to be with me."

"And I couldn't. Because I thought you were wrong."

"I believe in being loyal."

"So do I. But it depends on what you're loyal to." He looked out the window. There was just enough of that damn sunlight to give his eyes a glow that made him look eager and young.

"I'm not a great writer, Ange. I wanted to be. Hell, when I started I wanted to be Tolstoy and Fitzgerald and Shakespeare and Hemingway all rolled up into one. But I'm not a genius. What I am is a soap opera writer. And I'm a damn good one. Partly because I take it very seriously. So I give my loyalty to the show I write and the audience who watches it. And so do you. Or at least, you always did until you allowed yourself to be overcome with a lot of schoolgirl sentimentality about Jesse."

"I made a professional judgment . . ."

"You made a personal judgment. Because you loved Jesse. Like a lot of other people. And you all got hurt."

"We had a lot of reasons for loving her."

"I'll admit that Jesse could be charming, and warm, and very generous—when things were going her way. But she was a spoiled brat. And what drove me crazy was that you are one of the brightest women I've ever known and you couldn't see it."

"She gave me . . ."

"I know, I know." He got up and started pacing. "She gave you your start. You wouldn't be where you are today without her. I've heard the legend a thousand times. But what I never heard about was what you did for her. Like keeping her a leading lady years longer than she actually was one. You covered her ass, Ange; you shot her best side, you lit her like an angel, you tailored her stories to hide her age. She owed you as much as you ever owed her."

I was losing the fight but I couldn't give in. "Jesse was the heart of the show. *Bright Tomorrow* never recovered from losing her."

"We never recovered from losing you, you idiot. You were worth ten of Jesse but you never knew it."

I got up and went to him.

"Why the hell didn't you say that to me back then?"

"I tried, but you were too pigheaded to listen."

This time I reached up and kissed him.

When we finally came up for air he said a little breathlessly, "I'm not apologizing for this one."

"Neither am I."

"But I am getting out of here."

"If that's what you want."

"The truth is, I don't know what the hell I want."

"I know."

He gave me a brotherly peck on the top of my head before he left.

When StarsAnswerFone called three minutes later the operator sounded confused. "Are you sure you still need our wake-up calls, Miss Da

Vito? You sound real perky."

I told her to have a lovely day.

What the hell, perky always used to work for Doris Day.

Chapter
Sixteen

My happy blur lasted all the way to the office and well into the morning. I was especially nice to Nan, who was clearly expecting me to hand her her head on a plate for telling on me. I made a mental note to myself to confuse Nan more often. It was good for her character and fun for me to watch.

Then at around eleven o'clock I got a call from the front-door guards. It seemed that a Mr. Raymond St. Clair was in the lobby making a fuss because his old friend Charlie, who would have let him into the building in a flash, was not on duty. Instead there were a bunch of strangers who did not recognize him and refused to believe that he had once been the hottest sex symbol in daytime television.

I raced downstairs double time. We still had a small but determined press corps camped outside the building, and I wanted to get to Ray before the vultures did. In his heyday, there was nothing Ray loved more than giving interviews.

I shouldn't have worried. Vinnie and Mitch had vouched for him. By the time I reached the first-floor hallway, Ray was happily holding court, surrounded by a group of the old-timers who remembered him. News of his presence had probably spread through the studio like wildfire.

When he saw me, he separated himself from his throng of admirers.

"I apologize for the scene, Petkin," he boomed. "I had not counted on the kiddie constabulary."

"A security measure. After our recent tragedy. What can I do for you, Ray?"

"I thought of something concerning that case of yours and I thought I'd better hie me over here. Perhaps I could have phoned, but . . ." He grinned a little sheepishly. It was a lame excuse and he knew it. The truth was, he hadn't been able to resist coming back to what had once been the center of his universe. Not after I'd given him a role of importance in our splashy crime. For a brief moment I wanted to kick myself for not having gone to the library for my history lesson. The last thing I needed was Ray St. Clair in the studio advertising my continued efforts at detective work at the top of his lungs.

Then I looked at him again. He was nattily turned out in a Douglas Fairbanks, Jr., ensemble of navy blazer and gray slacks, with a pocket hankie that matched his ascot. He was also wearing, if I was not mistaken, a very light application of Max Factor erase cream under his eyes. I thought of those damn scrapbooks and his mausoleum with the pink lighting.

"Don't be silly, Ray," I said. "Of course you should have come over. The place has changed a lot. Would you like the grand tour before I take you up to my office?"

"Thank you no, sweet one. I've seen most of my old pals. Except dear Tommy Props of course. And I . . . well, perhaps this might not be a good time."

"Tommy is out today," I said. It seemed to me that Ray was relieved.

"It's just as well. Having cast myself as Watson to your Sherlock, I have much to impart . . ." He lowered his voice to a stentorian sotto voce which could be heard three buildings away. Ray may not have been a very good actor, but he was always a loud one. "I have been brooding on your gold lamé posies, my dear, and I have remembered a tidbit that I fancy will be of use."

I could see ears pricking up all the way down the hall. Quickly, I got him upstairs and into my office before he could spill any more.

Once we were behind my closed door he arranged himself gracefully in my chair, angling his face away from the direct light.

"About those roses," he began importantly. He was definitely planning to milk his time with me for all it was worth. "I remembered after you left that there had been some uproar in the making of them. As I told you, the whole point of the dream sequence was that everything in it was supposed to match the real wedding—only in gold. With most of the props that wasn't hard to do, a bit of paint took care of it. But Tommy couldn't find any long-stemmed gold roses that looked like the ones Jesse would be carrying in her real bouquet."

I didn't like where this was going.

"The roses were considered props, not a part of her costume?" I asked cautiously.

"Getting those roses was Tommy's responsibility. He shopped everywhere: millinery stores, trim and fabric warehouses. He went all over the Lower East Side, but there just weren't any for sale. Then he tried spraying some artificial white roses with gold paint but they looked terrible and Jesse threw a fit. So the producer decided to cut the bouquet in both shows. But Jesse really hit the roof at the idea of marching down the aisle without flowers."

Then he said what I didn't want him to say.

"So the night before we taped the fantasy sequence Tommy stayed up until dawn making twelve long-stemmed gold lamé roses for Jesse. He gave them to her on the set just before dress rehearsal. We all applauded as I recall. Well, you know the way Tommy worshiped Jesse."

I knew.

"I'm not saying that Tommy took the roses. But they certainly could have gone back to the prop department after we shot the show. It was where they belonged."

I nodded.

Ray sighed. "I keep remembering the way Tommy always made sure the coffee was hot when Jesse had to play one of her endless kitchen scenes. She'd told him once that the details were what gave her her inner truth. The Actors' Studio was very big back then and I think she was quoting some hairy female who never shaved. Jesse herself never believed any of that swill, but dear little Tommy used to bring that steaming coffee pot to her like it was the Holy Grail. . . . What the hell was that?"

He broke off because there was a crash from Nan's office. For a moment I sat frozen, making no move to investigate. I knew it wasn't Nan wallowing around in there because I'd told her she could take an early lunch. The panic I'd thought I'd buried on the previous night started kicking in again.

"Angie?" It was Ray at my side. "Would you like me to call the Keystone Cops?"

He was looking at me with more concern than fear, and I had an unpleasant picture of myself scared of shadows in my own office. I got up quickly and opened the door which joins Nan's office and mine.

"What happened?" Ray joined me in the doorway. I pointed to a picture, the glass broken, which was lying on the floor. Nan keeps a small photo gallery of her friends and family on a round table near our door. A framed shot of Howie, her husband, the kids, and the family poodle, Fierce, had fallen off it.

"It was probably something freaky like the building shaking or sound vibrations; we're very near the subway," I said bravely.

But I was thinking that neither Nan nor I ever locked our office doors during the workday. Maybe it was time we started.

Chapter
Seventeen

The picture incident made me jumpy. So perhaps it was my overactive imagination that made me feel that someone was watching me as I escorted Ray back downstairs—and on and off for the rest of the day. At first I was spooked by it. Then I started to get mad. I resent feeling spooked in my own studio. I decided I was damned if I was going to be intimidated by some klutz who went around knocking down pictures while eavesdropping. Unfortunately it might also be the same klutz who went around shooting people.

I left a note for Nate that he was to see me before he left for the day on pain of death. Then I dawdled around in the control booth after taping until everyone else had gone home. Across the gloom of the soundstage I could see that the light was still on in the prop room, meaning that Nate was still there. Finally I marched over to confront him.

He'd also been stalling, taking too much time to pack up the surgical instruments that had been used in a hospital scene.

"Why was Tommy out today?" I asked as I pulled the door shut behind me.

"I told him to stay home. He really was sick, Angie. It's not . . ."

"Don't lie to me, Nate. I want to help him."

Nate sighed. "I told him to stay home because he was drunk. He's been on a bender ever since Gregg was killed."

"Where are the rest of the roses?"

He dropped a scalpel. "What roses? I don't know what you're talking about."

"Cut the crap, Nate. I know Tommy saved the gold lamé roses he made for Jesse. And I know one of them is missing. I also know that's why you've been acting like something out of a bad cop movie for the past week. The good news is that so far the police don't know about any of this. So give me the rest of the roses."

Nate bent down to retrieve the scalpel, which gave him a few seconds to consider what I'd said. Then he straightened up and looked me in the eye. "There is no 'rest.' "

"There has to be. There was a whole bouquet of those roses."

"But Tommy only had one. I swear on my mother's grave, Angie."

I felt something jagged in my chest start to melt.

"You mean there are eleven of those little suckers still floating around?"

"I've only seen the one Tommy had. He kept it in his desk drawer with Jesse's picture . . . Were there more?"

"A dozen originally."

"But that means . . ." A huge relief-laden smile crossed his face as the light dawned. "Holy shit.

If there were more of those roses, then Tommy's in the clear."

"Not completely."

"Sure he is! Come on Angie, there were twelve of those goddamn roses, right? That means eleven other people could have had one. Potentially. And any one of them could have killed Gregg. Jesus, I haven't felt this good in days."

"Before you break out the champagne there are still a few loose ends. Like Tommy had a strong motive for killing Gregg."

"Everybody who knew Gregg had a motive for killing him. You and I could come up with eleven names easy."

"Okay, then what about Tommy's rose? Are you sure it's gone?"

His smile faded. "I tore this place apart looking for it."

"How long has it been missing?"

Nate swallowed hard.

"The last time I saw it was the morning before Gregg was killed."

It was my turn to swallow hard.

"Are you sure? How can you pinpoint it? You said he kept it in his drawer."

"Angie," said Nate gently. "I know I saw it because Tommy was showing it to Jeffy Dowers. The kid hangs out in here whenever he can get away from that bi . . . his mother. Sometimes Tommy even lets him help when we have to work with papier-mâché. Tommy says he's got a real gift."

I allowed myself to fantasize briefly but pleasurably about Bitsy's reaction if her son the star should one day decide to become a prop man.

"Tommy was showing the kid how he glued in the petals. And then Jeffy had to rehearse and Tommy left the rose out on his desk. I figured he forgot it. Next day when I came to work it was gone. I didn't think anything about it until I heard about the rose they found on Gregg. I haven't thought about anything else since."

There had to be a way out.

"Could anyone else have gotten into this room besides you and Tommy? Maybe someone else has a key?"

"When I started to work for Tommy, he had to have his key copied for me. He didn't even have a spare."

"Maybe Tommy forgot to lock up that night. And the murderer went into the prop room . . ." The look on Nate's face would have told me I was grabbing for straws if I hadn't already known it.

"I do the locking up," he said. "I could have forgotten, but . . ."

I didn't think he had forgotten either. Nate gives new meaning to the word "reliable."

I must have looked as defeated as I felt, because Nate began grabbing at straws.

"Tommy could have brought the rose home that night," he said. "Or he could have decided to throw it away. Anything could have happened to the fucking thing."

I smiled at his effort and didn't point out what we both knew. Tommy had kept that rose in the

Jesse Southland Memorial Drawer for years. There was no reason to hope that he'd suddenly decided to take it home or dump it on the night before the murder. No reason except that Nate and I just couldn't live with the idea of Tommy Props as a killer.

Nate was looking at me.

"I don't know what Tommy told the cops about the rose," he finally said. "I don't even know if they've questioned him yet. Today was the first day he's been here since Gregg was killed and I sent him home . . ." He trailed off. I waited.

"Tommy's been real good to me," he started up again. "Couple of times I was short last year when the baby was born, Tommy bailed me out for the mortgage. . . ."

"So you lied to the police when they asked you if you'd ever seen the rose before."

"I figure if Tommy wants them to know about it, it's his business to tell them."

"I think that's called obstruction of justice and I'm not sure how much trouble you can get into for doing it."

The lines of worry in Nate's face deepened for a second, then he shrugged.

"I guess you and I will find out together, won't we?"

I considered denying that I was doing any obstructing of my own but I knew it would be a waste of time. I nodded and turned to go.

"By the way, Angie," he said casually as I opened the door, "you think you could solve this thing by next Thursday? Before noon?"

I whirled around.

"You didn't," I said.

Nate was grinning widely.

"Come on. Tell me you guys don't have a pool."

"On something as big as this? The pot is already two hundred bucks. My money's on you finding the killer sometime next Thursday morning. If you come through, I'm going to take my wife out to dinner. Got the place all picked out. Real romantic. I figure my sex life should pick up for at least six months. So how about it?"

It made me laugh. But only for a moment. Because as I left the prop room and started walking across the darkened soundstage the all-too-familiar feeling that I was being followed came back stronger than ever. I forced myself not to go back to Nate. But I couldn't help remembering that the guards were gone for the day. When I finally reached the heavy door to the hallway I yanked it open and closed it fast with an unreasonable sense of relief.

The hallway was cold, empty, and dim. At night in the Broadcast Center we turn the heat down and the overhead lights off as economy measures. There was a shaft of light at the end of the hall coming from the lobby. As I hurried toward it I contemplated calling the police.

I was in way over my head. And I knew it. If there's one thing I hate it's amateurs. In my business I get to meet lots of them. The proud papa who tells me his daughter Myrtle is a great natural performer because of the way she belts out "Memories" at the family picnic. Or the woman whose best friend Rose really should write a soap opera because her life is one, hah hah. Every time I'm faced with one of these arrogant jerks I have to repress a lecture on the many years of training and dedication which separate the professional from the dilettante. And now here I was, assuming that I could out-detect the professional cops. Me and Miss Marple. Talk about arrogant.

Besides, I was tired of being scared. Tired of dreaming about gold lamé roses. And very tired of asking questions for which there seemed to be no answers. Except the ones that were breaking my heart.

It was time to call the police, to ask for Teresa, or whoever was covering for her if she was still on her mysterious trip, and spill. I walked into the lobby, which was brighter than the hallway because of the illuminated ABN logo on one wall. I checked my watch in the reflected glow of our corporate symbol. Nine o'clock. Late in the day but still early enough to call my friendly local guardians in blue. Somebody would be there. Wasn't there something in the policeperson's code about neither snow nor sleet keeping them from their duty? Or was that the postpeople? All I had to do was go back inside the studio, walk to the pay phone at the end of the hall, find a quarter in my purse, and . . .

And hand my friends over to the authorities. Tell Teresa that Tommy had a missing rose and he had hated Gregg. That Anna Martin might have had at least one rose and, if she'd flipped again, a motive. That Lucy Stone said Linda McCain had a motive. That Lucy herself had a motive. That anyone working on *Bright Tomorrow* could have stolen Marc's key. That Chrissie could have stolen it.

Teresa didn't know these people the way I did. She didn't know how utterly impossible it was that any one of them could have committed a murder.

Besides, Nate and the guys on the crew had a pool going on me.

I walked out of the building. And went home— where I didn't make a single phone call.

Chapter
Eighteen

The next morning there was no time to ponder what I had done: at nine-thirty Larry and I had a long story meeting.

Every three months we have to go through this ritual. It's an all-day marathon in which we pitch to our superiors at ABN the stories which we would like to run on *Bright Tomorrow* for the next four to six months. What we want out of this little exercise is a speedy okay for our well-conceived ideas so we can get the hell back to work. What we get is input. Hours and hours of input. From gifted folk like Lucy Stone and Linda McCain. And, once upon a time, God help us, Gregg Whithall.

Nor do we get to endure this nonsense in the more than adequate writers' office in our studio. No indeedy. For this treat we have to schlepp over to ABN East Coast headquarters, a hideous, three-cornered skyscraper which disfigures a good portion of Sixth Avenue. It is known to those of us in the business as The Bermuda Triangle—The Triangle for short—for all the obvious reasons.

My cab pulled up at The Triangle just as Larry was getting out of his. He was clutching his briefcase, looking grim. Like most head writers, Larry would rather have his toenails removed with hot pincers than go to a long story meeting. He brightened up a bit when I called out his name, and he hurried over while I paid off my driver. Then the memory of our last meeting must have come back to him because he stopped as he was bending down to give me the standard peck on the cheek and stood there looking awkward.

"Relax. It was just a little light necking," I whispered as I reached up to plant my own kiss somewhere in the area of his chin. "Very nice, but not exactly grounds for a scarlet *A* on the forehead."

He smiled but not a lot.

"Ange, didn't your mother teach you never to tell a man that it was 'very nice'?"

"No. But then she never thought landing a man was much of an accomplishment. Not like getting a booking on *The Ed Sullivan Show*."

I thought I was being funny. But Larry looked at me sadly. "I know, Ange." He gave me a quick, affectionate squeeze before he turned and started up the wide marble stairs that led to the entrance of The Triangle.

"Something bad is going to happen," Larry muttered after we had signed in and were skidding across the glossy marble floor of the lobby. "Lucy and Linda are out for each other's blood and they're going to do something nuts. I can feel it."

I dodged the spray from the fake waterfall on the right wall.

"What can they do to us that hasn't already been done?" I soothed. "Remember the time

Gregg decided we needed steamier sex on the show so he made us sit through a screening of *Body Heat*?"

It had taken the better part of an afternoon. Every time Kathleen Turner flared her nostrils, Gregg had stopped the movie and made us sit through a slow-motion replay of the moment.

"This is going to be worse than steamy sex," Larry said gloomily. "Or Kathleen Turner's nostrils," he added, having read my mind.

Years of experience have taught me to respect Larry's intuition. So I brooded as we climbed into the elevator and began the stomach-lurching ascent to the thirty-second floor.

As usual our meeting was scheduled in the main conference room. This is a deceptively cozy chamber furnished with large couches and pretty flowered drapes. The conference table is a Danish modern affair which looks like something you'd use for a neighborhood brunch on Sunday in New Rochelle.

But just when you've been lulled into a false sense of security, you notice the bank of monitors on the wall which can tap into any ABN studio on either coast. And the four phones, two fax machines, and large wall chart which tracks the ratings—weekly, monthly, and overnights of all ABN shows—in crimson and black. Blood has been shed in this cheery room. And careers have died.

Larry and I were early. We arrived as the waiters were setting out the coffee and miniature oat bran muffins which are the specialty of the executive dining room next door. The muffins are nasty little things that taste the way sawdust looks.

Larry wandered over to stare moodily out the window, while I went to the phones to call the studio. Eric was line producer for the day and I'd briefed him very carefully. But I still like to stay in touch when I know that I'm not going to be in the control booth for taping.

Nan picked up her phone on the first ring. Which threw me.

"What's wrong?" I demanded.

"It's this upbeat positive attitude of yours, O noble leader, which is such an inspiration to those of us who toil in your cause."

"Allow me to rephrase. Why the hell are you pouncing on your phone the second it rings?"

There was an ominous beat at the other end of the line.

"I'm waiting for word about Anna Martin. She did not show up for rehearsal this morning. Don't yell," she added before I'd had a chance to draw breath. "We know she's been in the area. There was a sighting of her at six-thirty A.M. We figure she finally caught that stray cat that has been hanging around and took it over to her animal rescue group on the East Side. You know how obsessed she's been ever since Gregg let that dog die."

"Call Teresa," I said.

"What?"

"Detective O'Hanlon. She should be back from

her trip by now. Call the precinct."

"Angie, I really don't think . . ."

"That's where you'll find Anna. She's talking to Teresa. Make the call and get back to me."

I gave Nan the number and hung up just as Larry called me over to the window.

"Take a look down there," he said, pointing to the distant sidewalk below us.

From the thirty-second floor it was hard to see the street below us. But you couldn't miss the two stretch limos which raced each other to the curb in front of the ABN building. A tiny blob emerged from each. One was distinctly bigger than the other. The smaller was a rather violent shade of pink. After years of traveling everywhere together, Lucy and Linda had ordered separate limousines.

Larry and I watched the blobs skirt each other warily and head for opposite sides of the stairs. There was heavy weather ahead at The Bermuda Triangle.

The phone rang and I picked it up to hear Nan sounding cross.

"I hate it when you're right," she said. "You're full of yourself for days."

"I take it Anna is at the police station?"

"She was. She just waltzed into her rehearsal two minutes ago. It seems that your buddy the detective wanted to ask her some questions."

"How is Anna? Is she upset?"

"I haven't noticed. She knows all her lines and she's not bumping into the furniture. What more can you ask from an actress? Can you think of any reason why Nate Bernstein desperately, urgently seeks an audience with you?"

I could think of many reasons. None that I cared to discuss.

"No. I can't."

"I also hate it when you're being secretive. I suppose you can't think of any reason why the good detective wants to speak with you either?"

"Teresa?" First on my list of people with whom I did not want to have discussions. "Tell her I'll get to her when I can. And while you're at it, ask her to lay off my actors during the workday. Explain to her that there is a tradition that says the show must go on. Also several millions of dollars in advertising revenues which will be lost if we continue to suffer from police harassment." I slammed down the receiver and turned to see Larry staring at me.

"You said you were going to level with the police," he said.

"I am," I said. And was mercifully saved from an in-depth grilling about the exact timing of such a conversation by the arrival of Lucy Stone.

In her zeal to be first on the scene, she must have sprinted all the way from the elevator because she was panting openly. And her beret, which had been designed to perch rakishly over one eye, had slipped down and was covering the left side of her head like a large pink earmuff. She entered the room without a word and rushed to the head of the conference table where she slammed down her tapestry-covered briefcase. Next she fought her way out of her pink woolen cape and draped it over the corresponding chair. Gloves and a scarf followed. Then, having staked out her territory, she allowed herself a mean little smile and left. Headgear hanging on precariously.

Larry shook his head. "There are some characters you just can't write," he murmured. "No audience would buy them."

Linda walked in next, looking as cool as Lucy had looked frazzled. She saw Lucy's paraphernalia planted in the power spot and shrugged slightly before turning away to pour herself a cup of coffee and look out the window.

After that, in fairly rapid succession the rest of the group showed up. They included Lucy's longtime, long-suffering secretary, Binky; Linda's secretary, Maria; Jimmy Chapman, ABN Liaison for Daytime; and Suzanne Melman, who is head of something called Writer Development for the network.

Nobody knows precisely what it is that the Liaison for Daytime does, which is probably why the highly salaried position continues to exist. Jimmy spends a lot of his time running focus groups and audience polls. The wisdom he gleans is supposed to help us formulate stories which will appeal to the popular taste and keep ABN ratings high. I don't think he's ever actually watched any of the daytime lineup, relying instead on something called "my gut" and, of course, his test results.

Suzanne is supposed to act as talent scout and trainer for the new writers we constantly need in a medium that eats writers for breakfast. In my experience most of her hot discoveries turn out to be the dear friends of her dear friends who got her the job in the first place. However, the myth is that Suzanne has flair.

After two drinks Larry can do deadly imitations of both Jimmy and Suzanne.

Now, however, he turned on his considerable charm. He air-kissed Suzanne and did a manly shoulder clap on Jimmy before rushing over to help poor old Binky as she entered the room, attempting to balance a Dictaphone, a Power Notebook, a pile of scripts, a thermos of Lucy's special hazelnut-mocha decaf coffee, and a videotape. Larry managed a save as the tape slid off the top of the pile.

"Thank you," Binky gasped. "That thing arrived this morning by pouch from the Coast, and Lucy told me to guard it with my life."

I saw Linda eye the tape, a tiny frown briefly creasing her face. Then she moved to intercept Jimmy, who was seating himself at the table.

"Why don't we sit on the couches," she said smoothly. "So much more comfortable, don't you think?"

We dutifully settled ourselves, three each on the sofas, with Maria pulling up a small hassock for herself. When Lucy returned, her options for a seat would be the floor or solitary splendor at the table.

"Before anyone says a word, there is an idea I wish to plant," said Jimmy, leaning forward eagerly. Next to me I could feel Larry bracing himself.

"Nuns," Jimmy said triumphantly. And looked around at the rest of us for applause. What he got was bewildered stares. "We do a story about nuns," he said by way of explanation. "I feel it in my gut. Look at *Sister Act*. A blockbuster sleeper. Look at all those old Ingrid what's-her-face movies. This nun thing is fresh, it's new, but it also has legs. With a nun we cool out the family-values people because there's no sex. Maybe even get some parent groups because there's no violence. And all the testing indicates that God is going to be big in the nineties. I tell you God is mucho hot."

"What about a priest?" Larry asked before I could reach over to kick him.

Jimmy gave it four seconds of concentrated thought. "Frankly, guys who don't get laid are a turnoff. I'd rather stick with the gals. Call me a chauvinist," he added with a wink.

There were so many things I wanted to call him. But Lucy Stone walked in.

"Good morning, everybody," she sang out. She was without her hat and she was wearing a sugary smile. But her eyes above the smile were glittering dangerously. She looked around the room until she connected with Linda. There was an icy silence as the two women stared at each other. I'm so used to thinking of Linda and Lucy as comic relief that I tend to dismiss them as harmless. But at that moment I could see either one of them easily committing murder if it seemed like a necessary career move.

It was Lucy who broke the spell by turning to address the rest of us. "Sorry I'm late," she cooed. "But I know you'll all forgive me when I show you my surprise. Linda, love dove, you'll never be comfortable sitting on that silly couch."

She wafted over to the VCR, picked up the tape Binky had been carrying, and shoved it into the machine.

"I think you'll all be able to see better if you sit here at the table," she said as she settled into the chair she'd chosen for herself.

We moved ourselves to the table.

What unfolded on the oversize t.v. screen was an audition tape. Or it would have been if the actress featured weren't of the echelon that doesn't do audition tapes.

Stella Francis began her career falling out of her bikini top in beach blanket movies. She then moved on to co-star with a monkey on a short-lived sitcom in the early seventies. Most of the gags centered around the fact that the chimp was the bright one. After that, there were the years in which she was a regular guest on the game show circuit and hired out as a grand marshal in small town parades. Most recently she'd been on the home shopping network selling a line of her own cosmetics. No one had ever accused Stella of having talent, but somehow she'd always been a celebrity.

We sat through three scenes from *Chickie and*

the Chimp and a clip from Stella's infomercial on skin peels. Then Lucy stopped the tape.

"I know you're all just dying to know why I'm showing you this," she burbled.

This time it was Larry who reached over to kick me.

"You have just watched our new Claire Wingate," Lucy announced.

"No!" Larry and I said it simultaneously and involuntarily.

"I won't do it," I began.

But Lucy was looking past me at Linda. "What do you think, dearie?" she asked.

Linda was relaxed back in her chair, an expression almost like a smile on her face. "Bringing back Claire is a bad idea, Lucy," she said. "I've already talked to Michael Libson about it and he hates it as much as I do."

"Yes, he did hate it at first," said Lucy. She turned on the tape again. Now Stella Francis was wearing a copy of the famous skintight dress Marilyn Monroe wore to Jack Kennedy's birthday party. She was also singing "Happy Birthday."

"But then I suggested that we cast Stella Francis," said Lucy.

"Happy birthday, dear Mr. President Libson," sang Stella to an enraptured Michael Libson on the tape.

"Stella is one of Michael's oldest and dearest friends," said Lucy.

As one we all turned to Linda, who looked as if she was watching her life pass before her eyes.

That was when the phone rang.

"It's for you, Angie," said Binky.

"You'd better come over here," said Nan. "Anna Martin just fainted."

Chapter Nineteen

By the time I reached the studio, Anna was sitting up on the cot in the wardrobe room, sobbing. Marc and Boo were kneeling in front of her, with the Wild Turkey and a little vial of something which I took to be smelling salts between them. Magda was busily sewing snaps on a peignoir as if nothing was going on.

"Now Anna honey," Boo was saying, "if you can't stop I'm going to have to slap you." It didn't seem to be helping. I walked to the cot and indicated my willingness to take over. Anna looked up at me with huge, sad, very wet eyes.

"I swear I didn't remember about the roses, Angie," she gulped between sobs. "Sometimes there are things I can't remember. Because of the treatments I had. But then this morning when Detective O'Hanlon told me what Ray said, it all came back."

Someone must have told the police to question Ray. Maybe after he'd showed up yesterday at the studio. Thanks to me.

"I never would have taken one of those ugly roses. I wanted to forget that awful wedding show," Anna wept. "It was such a terrible time. Jesse screamed at me every day. Jesse was nice but she could be real hard on a kid, you know?"

I nodded that I knew, although I really didn't.

"My therapist says that's part of the reason why later on I . . . did what I did. It was wrong, I know, but that doesn't mean I killed Gregg."

I had the feeling I'd missed a few beats. So I grabbed at the obvious. "Anna, no one thinks you killed Gregg."

"Your detective does."

I really wished people would stop calling her my detective.

"She knows how much I hated him," Anna wailed.

"Because of that dog. Look, Anna . . ."

Anna choked back a sob. "That was evil," she said indignantly. "He really was an evil man. To let that poor little creature die just to hurt me. As if he hadn't hurt me enough."

The conversation was definitely passing me by. "When did Gregg hurt you?" I asked.

"When he dumped me." And she dissolved into new tears.

It took some more digging, but it finally emerged that it had been Anna Martin who was having the affair with Gregg that Jesse had discovered so many years ago. It had only lasted a few months, Anna sobbed, then Gregg got bored. I looked at her, sodden and hunched over on the cot in front of me, and thought about the far-reaching train of events she'd set in motion with her little fling. Our own personal, if somewhat unlikely, Helen of Troy. In a way it was awe-inspiring. I also found myself thinking that I was glad Jesse had never known that her nemesis was little Anna Martin.

Whether the police would deem a love affair that ended seven years ago sufficient motive for murder was a question I couldn't begin to answer. But it worried me for Anna's sake. Anna Martin is one of those people that other people always worry about.

Meanwhile I had a show to produce. Which meant getting Anna in shape to act. Somehow.

"Anna, would you like me to call your therapist?" I asked.

The effect was galvanizing. She stopped mid-sob. "Oh no," she said. She drew herself up to her full seated height. Even though she was perched on a first-aid cot, the pose had real dignity. "Poor Angie, you're afraid I'm going to go bananas, aren't you? Well, don't worry." Steel crept into her voice. "That's never going to happen again." She got up and walked to the door. "Please excuse me. I have a job to do."

"Anna, are you sure you're going to be okay?"

She stopped and turned in the doorway.

"I have three dogs and four cats at home," she said. "All of them highly unadoptable. I sponsor ten more strays in a foster-care program and I'm paying the bills to board twelve greyhounds that were slated to be killed because they couldn't race anymore. It's taken me a long time but I've finally found a reason for being an actress." She flashed me a dazzling smile. "I do this crap for my animals."

And the woman with four national fan clubs, three Emmys, and seven nominations made her exit.

Once I was sure Anna was on her feet—and performing more than usually brilliantly—I hailed a cab and raced back over to Sixth Avenue to try to pick up what I could of the writers' meeting, only to learn from Larry that they had just adjourned. He offered to fill me in over a coffee-shop lunch.

The meeting had ended quickly because Lucy had won, hands down. After hearing that Michael Libson himself had put together the show-and-tell tape for his dear friend Stella, Linda had capitulated whimpering.

"By the end she was trying to kiss Lucy's toes," Larry reported. "It was hard to watch her grovel. I've always thought of Linda as the strong, silent type."

The Girls had then established a brief truce for the purpose of forcing him to jot down a few story ideas for Stella.

"They're determined to bring her on the show. It's going to be a real battle to stop them," Larry said wearily. As he picked at the mushroom omelette he wasn't eating, I reached across the table and took his hand.

"You've got so much going on right now. Want to duck out of this war and let me handle it?"

"You mean let you go to the mat for both of us?"

"I'm your producer. It's my job to go to the mat.

Besides, I'm the one who likes to fight, remember?"

He pulled his hand away gently. "Don't make it too easy for me to wimp out on you, Ange. I said I'd back you and I will."

So we discussed ways and means. And finally came up with a game plan which consisted mostly of stalling the story as long as we could and ultimately threatening to quit if we had to.

"Stella might refuse to play the part if I wrote Claire as a child molester," Larry offered as we did battle for the check.

"Make that a child molester with a terminal disease."

We were so hard up, we actually tried to laugh at that.

Out on the street Larry said he was going to walk for a bit and helped me into a cab.

"Have you spoken to your detective friend yet?" he asked.

"What with one thing and the other I haven't had a lot of free time today."

"Ange, just do it and get it over with."

"I intend to," I said as the cab pulled away from the curb. And I did. Sooner or later.

Chapter Twenty

Back at the studio everything was moving along serenely. I deliberately stayed away from the soundstage because I didn't want Eric to feel that I was breathing down his neck. One of the worst things a boss can do, in my humble opinion, is delegate authority and then take it back.

So I was trying to be as unobtrusive as possible when Nate Bernstein suddenly materialized at my side.

"Sorry," he whispered as I jumped about two feet in the air.

"Damn it, Nate . . ." I started, but he put his finger to his lips.

"Hush," he said.

Which did stop me. I'd never heard anyone say "Hush" who wasn't Bette Davis.

Nate cast a wary glance down the hall and muttered out of the side of his mouth, "Thupxymif-tosip." Or words to that effect.

"Nate, what is this? First you try to give me a coronary, then you start speaking in tongues. I do not need this today."

"There's something you have to see," he said in a low voice. There was a haunted look in his eyes. He checked over his shoulder like a character in a grade B Hitchcock movie and motioned to me to follow him. "Come on," he said urgently.

Our destination was the soundstage. Once we were inside, Nate pressed himself against the door where the shadows hid him and motioned to me to do the same. We stayed this way for almost a minute watching the dress rehearsal which was in progress. Then when there was a break and everyone was focused on moving to a new set, we ran to the prop room.

"Nate, I'm losing my patience," I warned once we were inside. But he simply put his finger to his lips again and opened Tommy's desk drawer.

"Look," he whispered.

Inside the drawer, lying in plain view, was a gold lamé rose.

"How?" I asked after a moment.

Nate shook his head wordlessly.

"Maybe Tommy . . . ?"

"He's still out on sick leave."

"It must have been in here all along. You must have missed it."

For an answer Nate just looked down at the rose. It was a theatrical prop, oversize, and very gold. Not the sort of item you'd miss. Especially if you were searching for it the way Nate said he'd been searching.

"When did you find it?"

"It was here when I came in this morning," Nate whispered. He stared at it with revulsion as if it might turn itself into something slimy that slithered. Then he turned away from it with a shudder.

"Angie, up till now I haven't wanted to know who killed Gregg."

"Because you were afraid it might have been Tommy."

"I didn't want to think it, but . . . You weren't working here when that lady from the dinner theater called and told him about the accident. He got crazy drunk, Angie. He went back there . . ." Nate gestured toward our locked weapons cage on the far wall. ". . . and he took out one of the pistols. He kept saying that Gregg had killed Jesse and now it was time for justice to be done. I finally calmed him down, but it scared the shit out of me." Nate closed the desk drawer carefully. The golden rose slowly disappeared from sight. "Tommy got crazy again when he heard that Gregg wanted to bring Jesse's character back on the show. So when I realized that rose was missing, I figured that . . ."

"That this time he might have done it," I filled in the blanks for him.

"But then this morning the damn thing turned up again. And now I don't know what to think."

"Neither do I. But maybe . . ." I broke off because something was starting to come clear.

"Maybe what?"

"Maybe I do know the right way to think. Don't try to understand," I added hastily as Nate's eyes started to glaze over. "I know what I mean. And I've got to go."

"But the rose . . ."

"Will not get up and walk. Trust me."

I made my escape over his protests, went to the wardrobe room where I said to a startled Marc, "Tell Teresa O'Hanlon about your key. Today." Then I grabbed a sweater off one of the costume racks, and left the building.

If you count the day they had to haul me out on a gurney because I had appendicitis, it was only the third time in my career that I'd abandoned ship without telling anyone where I was going. But I had to do it. It was walking time.

Chapter
Twenty-one

Exercise is not something I have ever done voluntarily. Once, when I was about six, Mama decided that The Singing DaVito Sisters should also dance. Connie dutifully learned the routine and went on stage to tap her little heart out. I inched behind her and refused to sweat.

But even I understand that every once in a while when you have something major to contemplate, you need to get away from walls and furniture and start walking.

So I walked and contemplated.

I realized that I'd been making a big mistake in the way I'd been looking at our murder. I'd been viewing it as a puzzle, so I'd been collecting random pieces of information which I hoped would fit together in a logical fashion. But a murder isn't a puzzle. It's a story. And any good story, as Larry is forever telling me, starts with the characters. Characters who are driven by emotions and needs that are not logical. So what did I know about the emotional, needy, and illogical character who had killed Gregg Whithall?

He or she was someone of great passion. Someone who had hated Gregg enough to take his life. And then humiliate him with a gesture: I remembered the cops snickering over his corpse.

And it was a reckless gesture. Made by someone

who cared more about making a statement than about being caught. And it was funny. Our killer had a sense of humor.

Then there were the roses. Obviously they meant something very special to someone. But what? And why play hide-and-seek with Tommy's rose? Why implicate him? Unless . . .

"Watch it, stupid," snarled a voice. In my trance I'd slammed into a young man wearing a neon sweatsuit and fearsome running shoes.

I was so absorbed I almost blurted out, "But what if the murderer was trying to protect Tommy?" But I'm a New Yorker. And we have a rigid protocol for street encounters. "Why the hell don't you look where you're going?" I growled and, without waiting for a reply, crossed the street against the light to get to a public telephone I'd spotted.

The phone didn't work. Naturally. Six blocks and two phones later I finally found one that did. And then realized that there was no way that I was going to get Tommy's phone number from information because I couldn't remember his last name. If indeed I'd ever known it. The only thing I was sure of was that it was not Props. I could have called Nan, who would have had it in her Rolodex, but I didn't feel like getting the third degree about where I was and what I was doing.

So I called the wardrobe room and asked for Boo, who has a Christmas card list of five hundred names and growing. His address book is the size of the world almanac and he always keeps it with him because he never knows when he's going to make another friend.

I was rewarded with the information that Tommy Props had been christened Thomas B. Callahan and that he lived in the wilds of Brooklyn. I hung up without answering any of Boo's urgent questions as to my whereabouts, hopped a cab, and headed south.

Chapter
Twenty-two

Tommy Props, a.k.a. Callahan, lived in one of the old working-class neighborhoods that still exist in pockets of Brooklyn and Queens. His home was the second in a string of square little houses on a block which boasted three similar strings. Aluminum siding was very big in this area and many of the small, carefully tended gardens displayed a statue of the Madonna ensconced in her own neon-blue grotto. "Mary on the Half Shell," my cousins and I used to call these artifacts when we were growing up. Our Nana had one in her front yard in Bensonhurst.

The cab found Tommy's home easily. In no time I was walking up his tidy fake flagstone walk to his front stoop. As I rang his bell, my heart began doing new and unfamiliar riffs on its usual rhythm. What if Tommy wasn't home? What if he was at home and hostile? What if he told me something I didn't want to know?

The door was opened by a woman who had to be Tommy's blood relative. His elfin features were slightly broader on her and his gray curls surrounded her face like a close-fitting cap. She looked at me with Tommy's bright blue eyes. But there the similarity stopped. Because there was none of Tommy's misty sweetness in her gaze. Or her voice. She established with brisk efficiency that

I was Tommy's boss, and she was his sister Peg who had just arrived yesterday from Tampa. To take charge. She agreed somewhat reluctantly to let me come in the house—after I wiped my feet.

I'd always pictured Tommy living in dusty bachelor squalor. So I wasn't prepared for the plastic covers on his imitation Louis XIV furniture or the rubber mats which covered his shag carpet. Peg explained with pride that this had been the decorating style of their late mother from whom Thomas had inherited the house some five years earlier. I had the sense that if Tommy had tried to strike out on his own with the decor, a hand from the grave would have appeared to forestall any changes.

I stumbled around a bit trying to find a delicate way to ask if Tommy was sober enough to talk to me, but delicacy was not required with Peg.

"Thomas is not drunk, if that's what you're asking. But it's very kind of you to come all the way down here to check up on him," she added in frosty tones which suggested that it was anything but. "You must be an unusual kind of boss."

"I . . . that is we all . . . think of Tommy as a friend . . ." I said, wilting quickly under a vintage New York stare. "I just wanted to ask Tommy a question."

"I'm afraid you can't do that. He's sleeping, and I won't disturb him. Doctor's orders."

"Of course," I said, fighting major disappointment. Peg moved to the door to show me out.

Then I had an inspiration. "He's so lucky to have you here," I said.

"Family is family," she said, but there was a shade less chill in her eyes.

"I mean, it's such a pity you can't be here all the time." I lowered my voice to a conspiratorial murmur. "Just between us, I've always felt that Tommy is the kind of man who needs a woman around to . . . well, to keep him out of trouble, so to speak . . ."

"Bless the dear Lord yes, he's always needed a woman, has Thomas. If I've told him once, I've told him a hundred times he should have married. And there were plenty of girls, good girls who could have given him a home with children, that would have been happy to have him. But none of them could measure up to his great Jesse Southland. Not that she ever gave him more than the time of day. An actress she was, and from what I can make out, no better than she deserved to be. But then, that's a man for you."

"The weaker sex," I said, remembering hundreds of feminine conversations around the kitchen tables of my youth. For a moment, Peg looked at me blankly. Then she burst into a hearty laugh.

"Not to hear them tell it," she said.

"But that's because we're so clever in keeping it from them. Big men, hah." I managed a snort exactly like the one with which my Aunt Sofia prefaced all remarks concerning her husband, Aldo.

Sisterhood was achieved.

"Would you like some tea?" Peg asked. "And maybe some cookies? I'm afraid they're store bought."

I said I was dying for a good cup of tea.

Minutes later I was attempting to keep from sliding off the slick slopes of the couch while balancing a teacup and saucer, a plate of cookies, a napkin, and assorted cutlery.

"Has Tommy said anything to you about a gold lamé rose?" I asked after I'd finally managed to swallow several scalding mouthfuls of tea.

"Then there really is one? He was ranting and raving about how he should have told the police about one that he'd lost. But then it all got garbled up—something about someone who was lying for his sake and he'd get them in trouble. Or some such stuff."

So Tommy hadn't told the police. And he'd known Nate was covering for him. Or was it someone else?

"Did he say who was lying for him?"

"When Thomas has been drinking, I never listen to him. It just encourages him, Mother used to say."

"Well, when he was ranting and raving did a name come up?"

"Not that I can remember."

"Do you know if he's talked to anyone at the studio about the murder?"

"No. Miss DaVito, is Thomas in trouble?"

"I don't think so. Not anymore."

"But he was?" I wasn't quite sure how to answer. She sighed angrily. "The police thought he did it, the murder, didn't they? That's why Thomas has been making all this . . . fuss. They thought he committed murder because of Her."

No doubt who She was. The room was dominated by a large, framed blowup of Jesse's last publicity shot which hung on the wall over the faux mantelpiece.

Peg stood up. "I want to show you something," she said. She led me to a small china cabinet. Three shelves were crammed with those frightening little albino figurines with the big heads and the bulging eyes that are sold in card shops. Precious something or other, I think they're called.

But on the top shelf, all by itself, in what was clearly the place of glory, was an article I recognized. It was Jesse's coffee pot. The pot which she had used as Claire. According to legend she and Tommy had gone shopping for that coffee pot the day before *Bright Tomorrow* made its debut. And Jesse had used it for all those years.

Memories started flooding me, until Peg's sharp voice cut through.

"Can you believe it?" she demanded angrily. "Look what he's done to Mother's Precious Moments collection. Just to make a shrine for that silly coffee pot. And why? Because the great Jesse Southland glued it together and saved him from being fired."

That was a story I hadn't heard and it must have showed on my face.

"I guess you didn't know about that," said Peg. "Thomas never told anyone who worked on the show. Lord knows Mother and I heard about it often enough. It seems that one day Thomas had had a couple of drinks too many at lunch and when he was putting away his props he dropped the sainted Miss Southland's coffee pot and broke it. Well, he was fit to be tied. Because of her character being identified with this pot, if you can believe a grown man even saying twaddle like that.

"He tried to replace it, but it was out of stock. And he was afraid that someone would ask what had happened to it and then he'd be fired for drinking on the job.

"But she came to the rescue. Next day she found some company where she could order out-of-stock china. But it was going to take a few weeks for the delivery. So that night, after everyone else had gone home, she went back over to the studio, snuck into Thomas's property room, and glued the broken pot together so it would hold until the new one arrived. Then she did it up in wrapping paper and left it as a surprise." Peg reached into the cabinet and took out the coffee pot. "Here," she said with heavy sarcasm. "You can see the crack where her sacred hands did the gluing."

Jesse had done a great job. No way anyone would have known what had happened unless they'd been looking for it.

"It's the sort of thing Jesse would do," I said softly.

I could see her, slipping into Tommy's prop

room, fixing the coffee pot, and leaving it, like a parent leaving the Christmas stocking for her kid to discover in the morning. There was probably a note with it. Telling Tommy lovey that he must stop worrying this instant because this was their little secret and tomorrow she wanted to see a smile on his face.

"I don't care what anyone says: she could be the most generous, caring person in the world," I said. Beside me Peg sniffed her disapproval. I was supposed to help dish Jesse, not defend her. Bonding time was over.

"I don't like to be rude," Peg hinted as she held out her hand for the coffee pot. "But it might be better if you weren't here when Thomas wakes up."

I surrendered the coffee pot reluctantly. I had the feeling that I'd just learned something important, but I didn't know what it was.

The feeling nagged at the back of my brain during the ten minutes of rigorously polite pleasantries Peg and I exchanged as we waited for the cab I'd ordered.

It continued to nag as my cab sped back toward Manhattan and the Broadcast Center. But nothing came to me. Which wasn't surprising. Vague feelings had been nagging at me every night since the murder with no positive results.

After a while I stopped pushing and tried to concentrate on something totally useless. It's a technique Larry uses to jog loose writer's block. What he does is alphabetize his ancient record collection.

What I chose to do was count the number of blocks on my route which did not have at least one pizza stand.

When I got to eighty-seven I slumped back into my seat and admitted defeat. I'd gone to Brooklyn hoping that Tommy would give me a name that would dovetail with the character sketch I'd created. What I'd gotten was more confusion and some very hot tea.

Chapter
Twenty-three

The broadcast center loomed dark and lonely when I got out of my cab. I told myself firmly that I did not miss the guards and the cops.

The ABN logo cast weird shadows on the lobby wall. As I let myself into the building with my ID card, I wondered when the police would let us have our trees back. I'd always thought they were silly but at least they'd filled up the empty space. Then from the back of the lobby I heard sounds. For a second I froze. Then I thawed. I refuse to be afraid of anyone who is whistling the McDonald's jingle.

At the back entrance I found two members of the building maintenance crew hard at work smearing the dirt on our brass doors.

Each of the studios has its own janitor who does the daily pickup, but once a week at night there's an outside crew which comes in to give the entire building a heavy cleaning. I hated how pleased I was to see them.

"Are you guys just starting?" I asked hopefully.

"Yeah," said one, whose pocket monogram declared him to be Ramon. "We got the whole building to do."

"We finish here, we go up to the top and work our way down," offered his friend.

"Start at the top and work my way down to the bottom," said Ramon gloomily. "That's the story of my life." I figured he wasn't the one who had been whistling the McDonald's jingle. "You want to go up?" he asked.

"No thanks, I'm going into the *Bright Tomorrow* studio," I said and inserted my ID card into the lock to prove it.

My office desk was covered with the memos which had piled up in my absence. I skimmed them quickly, discarding the ones from Larry and Nan demanding to know where the hell I was, and earmarked the rest for attention first thing in the morning. The unedited tape of the day's show was also on my desk, neatly labeled in Eric's precise hand. He directed my attention to act four, scene two, in which he felt he'd gotten a particularly fine performance from Anna. I wondered how he'd feel if he knew that it was not he who had inspired her, but twelve elderly greyhounds.

Satisfied that there hadn't been any major disasters while I'd played hookey, I packed up my briefcase, grabbed my coat, turned out the lights, and left my office.

I waited until I got to the lobby to put on my coat—which was why I didn't realize earlier that I was still wearing the sweater I'd snitched from the costume rack. I considered just throwing on my coat, and bringing back the sweater the next day, but the chances were I'd forget it. Better to leave it on the doorknob of the wardrobe room where Marc would find it in the morning. I cursed briefly, then turned around and let myself back into the building. When I got home, I promised myself, I was going to have the longest, hottest bubble bath in the history of woman.

I was just leaving the sweater on the doorknob when I saw a light coming from Anna's dressing room.

I don't know why I didn't run. I think it was because I'd scared myself one time too many and I wasn't going to fall for another false alarm. Or maybe I need a keeper.

As I started toward the light, I told myself that Ramon and his colleague had decided to go for spiritual uplift and were working from the bottom to the top. I even whispered "Ramon?" as I approached the door.

The light went out—which might have scared me enough to make me run, except that the door was open and something inside the room caught my eye: a bag stuffed full of something which glittered slightly in the dark. Without thinking I went into the room and stooped over to pick up the canvas tote bag Anna had purchased at her last PETA rally. Then I heard a rustle behind me. I started to straighten up. But it was too late. There was an explosion of white-light pain in the back of my head. It brought me to my knees. More important, it seemed to be just the bit of extra prodding my brain had been needing. Because right before I passed out, I finally realized what was so important about that damn coffee pot.

Chapter
Twenty-four

When I came to, my recent epiphany was the last thing on what was left of my mind. At first I was too busy wondering where I was and why. I wasn't too strong on who I was, either. Finally the haze cleared enough for me to wonder if I'd died. Then, as the most painful headache of my life kicked in, I wished fervently that I had. Or still might. For several moments I clung to the floor and waited for a merciful God to take me home. When She didn't, I had to accept the fact that not only was I going to live, I was going to have to cope.

There was something wet and sticky on the floor around my face. It was also soaking my hair. Blood? I decided not to check. Clearly the first order of business was to get up off the floor and find someone who would make my head stop replaying the last moments of the "1812 Overture." And make it stop bleeding. If it was. Which I didn't want to know.

Plan A, which was simply to stand up and walk, proved to be an impossibility. Even the slightest movement produced a sickening swimming feeling. An alarming attack of nausea followed, and I went back to floor clinging for a bit. After a certain amount of experimentation I finally found a method of crawling which didn't seem to cause any major side effects. It wasn't the most efficient way to move, but the upside was that I wasn't going to vomit. Hopefully. I managed to get myself out of the dressing room and into the hallway without incident, although there were a couple of times when it was touch and go.

After that my memories get vague. I know that I reached the foot of the stairs, because that's where Ramon and his partner found me. I know that they called an ambulance and that I was taken off to the hospital to be checked out. I know that I asked that somebody call Detective O'Hanlon, but no one seemed to be listening.

The emergency room of a large metropolitan hospital is no place for a sick person. Especially in the wee hours of the morning when those citizens who like to inflict bodily harm on each other are at their most active. Fortunately, I wasn't paying too much attention to my surroundings when I arrived.

My mind was clearing although by no means totally clear. I lost a battle with a nurse who insisted on inserting an IV needle in the back of my hand, but it wasn't a fair fight. I was still having trouble holding a train of thought and she was used to subduing felons.

I'd filled out about three hundred forms and was starting to feel that I'd spent my entire life in the hospital when Teresa appeared. She began cutting through the red tape. Nurse Ratchett went off to spread joy elsewhere and a much nicer crowd of folk began patching me up. Even with Teresa expediting things it took another two hours to X-ray, stitch, bandage, and test me with trick questions about my name and that of my President. It was almost three o'clock by the time I was released. A cute young orderly allowed me to take my ice pack with me.

On the street I made a feeble stab at asserting my independence but was actually very glad when Teresa said she was going to take me home. Thinking still wasn't something I was doing very efficiently, but it had occurred to me that someone had been very serious about hurting me.

Chapter
Twenty-five

There were no unpleasant surprises waiting at my apartment building. Or in my apartment, which Teresa checked very carefully.

"Can you manage now, or do you need help with anything?" she asked.

There wasn't any part of my head, front or back, that didn't ache. I'd never known I could hurt so much.

"I should have told you about Marc's key," I said.

"Yes, you should have."

"I'm sorry."

"After this night, I'm sure you are."

"Are you going to charge me with something criminal?"

She seemed to consider it. "I don't think so," she said finally. "You probably did me a favor."

"I'm like that. How?"

The pain had become a condition of life; I could almost ignore it. Teresa hesitated before she answered me. Then I guess she figured that in my weakened state I wouldn't retain anything she said.

"If we'd known about the stolen key, my boss would have taken that as proof that the perp . . . the murderer was someone working on the show. An insider. Given that assumption, I don't think he would have let me have the extra manpower to continue surveillance on the outside of the building. And I wanted to continue." In my fog, the fine points of her explanation slipped by me, but I did latch onto one fact.

"You have a boss. I don't think of you as having a boss."

"Oh yes."

It was the way she said it. Her boss was the Lucy Stone of the police world. I saw a large, burly man with a mustache wearing Lucy's pink turban.

"I wonder if there are any good bosses," I said dreamily.

"I think it's time you got some rest," said Teresa.

"Yours doesn't like it when you act on your hunches."

"Remember they told you at the hospital to take some Tylenol."

"Especially hunches that take you off to the middle of nowhere. You were working on our case when you left town, weren't you?"

A slight pause. "Yes."

"How was the trip?"

"Inconclusive."

I nodded. Which was a mistake. I hadn't numbed out after all. "I've got to lie down," I said.

After Teresa left, I gulped down two Tylenol, and tried to avoid looking at myself in the mirror. For the first time in my adult life I wanted my mother.

As I was drifting off to sleep I remembered that I hadn't told Teresa about my big discovery.

When the StarsAnswerFone operator called I thought about screaming but decided it would take too much effort. The phone rang again as I was working on a game plan for sitting up.

"You are alive," said Nan.

"How the hell did you hear?" I moaned.

"I got it from Marc, who got it from Sylvia, who got it from Mitch, who got it from Vinnie, who got it from . . ."

"Spare me."

Her voice was suddenly full of concern. "That was a seriously stupid thing you did, Angie. Thank God you were hit on the head. It could have been a part of your body you use."

"Good-bye, Nan. I have to get ready for work."

"You are not to come into the office today. Do you understand me? We do not want you here. No one loves you."

"You're fired," I said as she hung up.

But she had a point. The journey across my bedroom to the bathroom was enough to convince me. The headache I had wasn't in the same league with the one I'd had earlier, but it was a contender.

On a cheerier note, I didn't look as bad as I felt. The bandage covering the knot on the back of my head was not overly intrusive. My face, except for red-rimmed eyes, looked about normal. Of course,

I was going to have to shampoo the rest of the dried blood out of my hair. I thought I remembered that there had been an instruction about not getting my head wet. I wondered if I should call someone and ask. But who?

Suddenly the whole thing seemed too complicated for a woman who had had only two hours of sleep. I told myself that I'd get over to the studio in time for taping and crawled back into bed to sleep.

But not for long. After about twenty minutes the phone rang again. This time it was Larry on the line.

"You promised me that you were going to talk to the police," he said in the tight voice which means his mouth has a thin white line around it. "You promised that you were going to allow them to do the job for which they, not you, are trained."

"I'm fine, thanks for asking," I said.

"Of course you're fine. It's the people around you who will die young."

"Gee. I thought I was the one who had her head bashed in."

There was a silence on the other end of the line.

"You'll never let anyone take care of you, will you, Ange?" he asked at last.

"Not unless I need it."

"Yeah. Get some rest, Angela. I'll talk to you later." And he was gone.

The conversation made me so uneasy that I almost called him back. But I decided to give him a chance to cool off. When Larry gets angry it's best to leave him alone for a while. At least it always used to be best.

Finally I fell into the kind of sleep that makes you wish you'd stayed awake. I dreamt in wild Technicolor about Gregg, and blood on the floor, and my faceless person who now had a face that I couldn't bring into focus. I was very happy when the phone woke me up. Only it wasn't the phone. It was the doorman's buzzer announcing Detective O'Hanlon.

Chapter
Twenty-six

Teresa didn't waste any time.

"I'm sorry to disturb you," she said before I had finished closing the door. "But I wanted to tell you that Anna Martin may be arrested."

"God. Where is she now?"

"At the station. We'll start questioning her as soon as I get back. She has waived her right to an attorney on the grounds that she doesn't feel she needs one. She does."

I let loose a string of the choicer phrases I'd picked up from the crew over the years. Teresa waited me out.

"What happened?" I finally asked. "Why do you suspect Anna?"

"We found ten gold lamé roses in a bag on the floor of her dressing room. Counting the one that is in the possession of the property master, that accounts for all twelve."

"How did you know about Tommy . . . ?"

"The little Dowers boy. Actually it was his mother who brought him to us."

Of course it was.

Teresa went on. "The theory is that Ms. Martin used one of the roses when she killed Mr. Whithall, and hid the others in her dressing room. Then last night, knowing that the maintenance crew would be cleaning her room, she came back to get them. You surprised her, so she hit you and, in her panic, left the roses behind."

"Here's another theory," I said. "Someone wanted to set up Anna and chose last night to do it because the maintenance guys would be sure to find the roses in her dressing room."

"That is not the way we are thinking at this time." Teresa did her deadpan delivery. But this time under the bland mask I could tell she was angry. She was being railroaded into arresting Anna and for some reason she wanted me to know it.

"But how do you explain the fact that Anna didn't take the roses home right after she killed Gregg?" I asked. "And why did she bring all ten of them to the studio when she only used one? And why . . . ?"

"She has a history of mental instability. At this point, that's how we're answering all questions of logic."

"Why? Do you have some kind of deadline for this investigation?"

Teresa hesitated. There was a big part of her that disapproved of what she was doing. But a bigger part of her disapproved of what she might be forced to do.

"Your network is a very powerful force in New York," she said. "The city wants to accommodate it. And your people want this case solved quickly. My boss was taken to lunch by two of the mayor's top aides, the police commissioner, and a Mr. Libson."

"Please say they went to California Dreamin'. Sorry. Bad joke."

Teresa's blank stare told me what she thought of comedy at this moment.

"What about your hunch?" I asked.

"It will take weeks to prove, and it will be expensive. My instructions are to put the pressure on Ms. Martin." She looked at me squarely. "Is she likely to crack and confess to a crime she didn't commit? She's already admitted to having memory gaps. My assessment is that she's suggestible and fragile."

As I said, Anna's one of those people everyone worries about.

"I'm not sure if Anna would confess," I said. "But I do know that getting arrested for murder will not be the kind of sexy scandal that will boost her TVQ. It could destroy her professionally."

Teresa nodded as if she'd been afraid of that. She looked at me silently for a long time. Then finally she spoke.

"We both know Ms. Martin didn't do it," she said carefully. "Do you have any ideas about who did?"

I was equally careful. "One. But it's very crazy."

"Tell me."

I told her. The instant I said the name, I wanted to take it back, but Teresa was already nodding. That was when I realized that she'd been thinking what I'd been thinking—probably before I'd started thinking it. "All along I've been feeling that there's something I know, or that I should know, about someone who's involved with the show," I added. "But so far I can't make the connection."

"Let's try to pinpoint it. Let's go over everything you know . . . or even think you know. Don't leave anything out—no matter how off the wall it may seem."

So I told her about my trip to Brooklyn and the tale of the coffee pot. About my dreams and my feeling that I'd been followed, particularly on the night that Nate and I talked about Tommy's missing rose—after which the rose miraculously reappeared. I found myself getting more and more excited as I talked. We were closing in on this thing. Solving the sucker. I knew Teresa was feeling it too.

"You seem to be saying that there's an accomplice. Someone who works on the show."

"I guess."

"I agree. That's been obvious from the beginning."

"Although . . ."

"What is it?"

"Just a feeling. That this whole scenario is more complicated than that."

"In what way?"

"I don't know." I tried to shrug it off. "Like I said, it's nothing more than a feeling. It probably doesn't mean a thing."

Teresa was watching me. "I doubt that," she said. "Your 'feelings' seem to be remarkably accurate. My problem is, time is running out."

"I know. What's going to happen to Anna?"

"I'll try to hold off on an arrest."

"And if you can't?"

"It won't last long."

"But it could be too long for Anna."

"Surely once she's cleared . . ."

"They'll still fire her. If she's arrested for murder there will be a momentary blip in her standing in some focus group or poll, and it will scare them. The people who run my industry do not have courage."

To say nothing of basic humanity. I could see Linda and Lucy tripping over each other in the race to fire Anna if they felt it would make points with Those Who Matter.

"There are some actors who could weather the mess and come back," I continued. "I don't know about Anna."

While I wasn't sure how much it cost to board twelve greyhounds, I had a sense that you couldn't swing it on an unemployment check. And I didn't know if Anna could survive failing her four-legged buddies.

But that was beside the point. Anna was innocent. Her only crime had been to fall for Gregg Whithall's smarmy charms seven years ago. And she'd already been punished for that.

Teresa was still studying me intently. When she spoke again, she weighed every word.

"There might be another way to go," she said. "A shortcut."

"Try it. Anything to get Anna off the hook."

"It would involve you."

That was a shocker. "Me? How?"

Teresa explained.

"I wonder why the name Benedict Arnold comes to mind," I said when she'd finished.

"If you're not comfortable with this . . ."

"I don't know how I feel. Give me a minute."

Teresa waited patiently while I digested the idea and all its ramifications.

At first I didn't like it much. But then I started thinking about the alternative. And all the people who had been hurt already.

"Could we do this today?" I asked.

"If you feel recovered enough."

"I'd like to get on with it. If I'm going to do it."

"Are you?"

"Yes."

She made a phone call and told someone, who was very reluctant to do it, to release Anna. Then she started out. She turned one last time at the door. "Angie?" she said. "Be careful. Remember what happened last night."

"I don't think I was in any real danger last night."

"Don't be so sure. If that trophy hadn't been such an awkward thing you could have been killed with it."

"What trophy?"

"Didn't you know? You were hit with an Emmy."

Anna Martin doesn't take her acting awards home. She stashes them in brown paper bags along with the kitty litter samples and the stacks of *Modern Dog* magazine she likes to read. I suppose it could have been worse. I could have been hit with a bag of kitty litter.

It wasn't until after she'd gone that I realized that Teresa and I had finally graduated to a first-name basis. She'd called me "Angie."

Chapter
Twenty-seven

I wanted to be as rested as possible, so I went back to bed for another two hours. Sleeping was something else again. Finally I quit trying. I cleaned myself up as well as I could, did a light makeup, dressed, and went to the studio.

As I'd anticipated, everyone descended on me. I had to tell and retell my story many times. And each time, I left little gaps in the telling which suggested that I knew more than I was saying. When I was called on it, I covered quickly and changed the subject. It was the best acting job I'd ever done, if I do say so myself. Maybe it had to do with having my head bashed in with an Emmy.

My next move was to go to the wardrobe room, where I found Magda and Boo, but no Marc. That was a minor disappointment. I'd been counting on Marc's genius for gossip. However, Boo was no slouch when it came to spreading the word, so I decided to go ahead.

"Boo," I said urgently, "do you remember yesterday when I called and asked you for Tommy Props' address and phone number?"

Boo nodded eagerly.

"You didn't tell anyone, did you?"

"No, sugar, I didn't." He was telling the truth. He hadn't realized that it was important. But now he was on red alert.

"Good," I said, sighing as deeply as I dared. I wondered if I should try for tears.

"Angie honey, are you okay?" Boo asked.

"I just wish I'd never gotten involved in this damn investigation, because now I have to see it through."

"See what through?" Boo could barely contain his excitement.

"Have you ever known something you didn't want to know?" I asked in a quavering voice. "About someone you loved? I've got to go."

I waited about twenty minutes for the village drums to do their thing, then I went looking for Nate. Luck was with me because I found him at the drinking fountain in the hallway. A nice public place. I asked him if he'd lend me his prop room key after work. When he asked why, I let myself have a tiny temper tantrum. He agreed with a reproach in his eyes that made me feel like something that crawled.

But it was worth it. Because as I went up to my office I could hear brains all over the studio putting two and two together and coming up with five. Angie knows something. And it has to do with Tommy Props. And she's going to check it out. Wonder what kind of injuries she'll get this time. Someone would probably start a pool.

It made me cringe to involve Tommy, but I comforted myself with the knowledge that it would all be over soon.

*　*　*

My plan called for me to stay very visible for the rest of the afternoon. Which was good, because I couldn't have handled being alone. I was too sad. Not scared, which would have been a reasonable, logical way to feel given what I was about to do, but sad. As if I was about to lose something precious. Dumb. But I couldn't shake it. I went back downstairs after the dress rehearsal and wandered around the studio.

The thirty minutes between dress and taping are a wild and woolly time on a soap opera. The whole show is bracing for performance. The hair and makeup people grab the actors for a last-minute pat with a powder puff or spritz of hair spray. Marc races after them, changing neckties and redoing jewelry. The director gives them notes. And the actors run lines. Compulsively. Alone and with their scene partners. Some pace, some smoke, some chew gum, but they all run their lines over and over, like members of a bizarre religious cult reciting their mantras.

And for some reason I had to be a part of it all. I had to check out the makeup room, look in on the wardrobe room, let myself absorb the tension through my skin.

It felt like I was storing up memories. Or saying good-bye. To what, I didn't know.

Finally we wrapped the show. I got the key from Nate and went back upstairs to my office as ostentatiously as I could. Following me, if anyone had wanted to, would have been a piece of cake.

In my office I walked around touching things. As if I would never see them again. I wanted to cry.

I waited fifteen minutes longer than I had to, just to make sure that everyone had gone home. Then I walked out into the hallway and began my journey to the soundstage. I remembered how eerie the empty building had seemed to me the night before. It didn't seem that way anymore. I kept waiting to get frightened, but I just felt sad.

Chapter
Twenty-eight

We have one permanent set on the soundstage, the kitchen which used to belong to Claire Wingate. Since it was our biggest and most elaborate set, we kept it after we lost the character. It's been redecorated and now is the kitchen of our obligatory doctor, but some of us will always think of it as Claire's kitchen. I walked toward Claire's kitchen.

The soundstage was dark; two weak work lights made yellow pools on the floor that were more like puddles. They did nothing to cut the gloom I walked through to get to Claire's set. Jesse's set. I stood in the darkness waiting.

Suddenly a large klieg on the side of the set went on. Startled, I turned to it, and was blinded by a ray of intense light surrounded by darkness. I turned away quickly. Then from behind the light, I heard a familiar, lilting voice.

"Olivier said you should be able to play any character with no makeup and no costumes, just your own talent."

I whirled toward the sound. She wasn't supposed to show up. I was waiting for her mystery accomplice. Or was I? Had I known all along that she'd be here? And how the hell had she done it?

She started moving toward me. Or rather, someone did. In the bright light all I could see was a silhouette coming at me. Of a body which was not, could not be, hers. But the voice was.

"I'm afraid I needed all the help I could get," the voice said. "Does that make me a bad actress, lovey?"

"No," I said. And as I answered the right voice coming out of the wrong body, I started to understand.

"Just not as good as Olivier?" she coached me as she continued moving.

I took a stab at it. "Olivier's audience wasn't living with him every day," I said.

I'd gotten it right. She giggled. She used to get fan mail on that light, charming giggle.

"That's right, lovey, I've been here every day right under your nose."

Any second now she'd move out of the light. And come close enough for me to see her face.

It was her eyes that I saw first. Beautiful lavender-blue eyes. Looking at me out of the fat, round face of a Hungarian wardrobe mistress. Lavender-blue eyes without the colored contact lenses that had turned them brown.

"Hello, Jesse," I said.

Jesse's eyes sparkled in Magda's moon face.

"Brava, Angie," she said. "At last. But it's taken you so long to get it."

"I could never keep up with you, Jesse."

"And yet, all these months, you were the only one who worried me. There were so many times I was sure you must have seen through poor Magda."

"No. I still wouldn't have recognized you, if you hadn't let me."

That pleased her. She lifted her hands to her hair. The fingers were fat sausages puffed beyond recognition, but the wrists were still tiny.

"Does this help?" she asked. She pulled out a couple of pins and released Magda's tight little knot into her own long bob.

I shook my head. It didn't do a thing for me because Jesse's signature white-gold mane had been dyed to Magda's dull brown.

"No. It doesn't help," I said. Which delighted her. She always loved to play games as long as she won.

"It took me almost a year to gain all the weight," she said. "I kept telling myself, if De Niro could do it, so could I. Was it the weight that fooled you?"

She was fishing for compliments now. The way she used to after a particularly good scene. I knew my cue.

"No, Jesse, it was your acting."

The moon face creased in a distortion of Jesse's lovely smile. "Was I that good?" she asked.

"You were brilliant."

"I never knew I could do character work," she said happily.

I wanted to lead her into the confession slowly. Draw the information out of her carefully. But I couldn't.

"Jesse, I can't believe this." I could hear the pain

in my voice and so could she. She turned away. "Why did you do it?"

"Kill Gregg? Why not?" She shrugged lightly, Jesse's graceful gesture encased in Magda's bulk.

"That's no answer."

She drew a deep breath.

"He took away my life. I'm an actress. No, damn it, I'm a star. That's all I am. All I ever wanted to be. He made me into a loser." In the half light her fleshy face grew dark with anger as she looked at some private vision I couldn't see. "They don't want a fifty-three-year-old leading lady, Angie. I guess I could have picked up a few crumbs. Extra and day player work. I used to feel so sorry for those people when they worked on my show. I insisted that our stage managers learn their names, remember that?"

"I remember. Go on."

"My money went fast. What there was of it. I'd never saved much because I thought I'd go on being Claire Wingate forever. So not only was I a loser, I was broke. And scared. You know what it's like to be scared like that, Angie."

"Yes, I do." And we both knew who had bailed me out.

"I couldn't hide the panic. Even I could hear it in my voice. People started refusing my phone calls. Who wants to talk to a desperate, out-of-work actress?" She gave me another travesty of a smile. "I wasn't working in a dinner theater in Ohio when I had my fatal accident. Want to know what I was doing?" She closed her eyes.

"I'd been hired by an ex-minister who had what he called a Motivational School. Based on the Jesus Pipeline for Dollars. I was teaching his self-esteem seminars. After my classes, I signed autographs and let my students paw through my scrapbooks. It's okay if you want to laugh."

I didn't.

"All that time I kept thinking about Gregg. And what he'd done to me. And I finally realized I had to do the same thing to him."

"You had to kill him."

"I had to make him into a loser. I had to take away his life the way he took away mine. Then I had to leave my mark on him. And get away with it."

"So you became Magda and hired on to the show. How did you set up the murder?"

"When I heard that he was bringing back Claire Wingate, I called him on the in-house phone. I used my own voice, which scared the hell out of him. And I threatened to go to the press if he didn't meet me downstairs in the *Bright Tomorrow* studio. I told him I'd be waiting for him in my old dressing room."

Steve's dressing room. Which had been Jesse's. "It had to happen there," she said.

Of course. It was the star dressing room.

"At first he was shocked when he saw me. Then he was revolted. He was so stupid, he couldn't even appreciate what a great acting job I was doing. What an incredible creation Magda was. I don't know how I could ever have . . ." For a moment she was lost in thought. Then she shook it off.

"In the beginning he tried to bully me. Then when he saw the gun—you're not going to believe this—he tried to seduce me." She giggled. "Isn't that wonderful? And he was so scared. As scared as I've been all these years.

"But the best part was when he finally realized what was going to happen. You should have seen the look on his face, Angie. There he was, naked, lying on the makeup table. My makeup table. Where we made love once. He was crying. And talking. Right up to the end he thought he could talk me out of it. He really was such a loser."

"And what about afterward?" I asked.

She looked at me blankly.

"You must have known that someone would be blamed for the murder."

She shrugged again. "I never thought that far ahead. In fact, the first time it occurred to me was when you started asking Steve about his dressing room key."

She frowned at me.

"You almost spoiled everything for me, Angie. There were only four of us who had those keys. That was too close for comfort."

"So you fixed it by stealing Marc's key."

"Wasn't that clever of me? I couldn't let poor Magda become one of four suspects."

So she'd thrown suspicion on everyone else. On people who had been her friends.

"But then you framed Anna."

The fleshy face twisted. "You know what the little bitch did to me. You heard her."

Yes, I had. And so had Magda. Quiet, unobtrusive Magda, who blended into the scenery. And heard everything. Magda, who hid in the prop room after she shot Gregg because she heard Chrissie come into the building. Magda, who had kept the prop room key that Jesse had used when she fixed the coffee pot. And it was Magda/Jesse who saw the rose on Tommy's desk and realized in horror that she'd just implicated him in the murder. So on impulse she'd grabbed it. And then later realized she'd made a mistake. And brought it back. Magda, the starring role in the show. Played by Jesse Southland.

"What are you going to do now, Jesse?"

"I think Magda will quit the show soon and fade away quietly. I'll be all right now that I've evened the score. I won't be a loser anymore."

"What about me?"

"I wish you'd known when to mind your own business, lovey," she said sorrowfully. And she reached into the large pocket of the dressmaker's smock Magda wore.

The next few moments were a blur of activity.

I'm not sure I believe Jesse would have used the gun she pulled out. Maybe I just don't want to believe it. But speculation about that is academic. Because Teresa and Hank were on top of her at the first sight of a weapon.

Jesse didn't struggle. Not after I told her that I

could and would testify against her if I had to. She just seemed to fade away standing in front of me. I watched the light go out in her lavender eyes. Taking the last of Jesse Southland with it. What was left was a sullen, dumpy little woman named Magda. If you saw her on the street you could tell from looking at her that she was a loser.

After Teresa and Hank had taken her away, I sat at the table in Jesse's old kitchen set. And I realized what I'd been mourning all afternoon. I'd come to *Bright Tomorrow* as a kid. Jesse had made me believe that what we did was magic. And somehow, through the years, in spite of everything, I'd continued to believe that. But now I couldn't anymore. So I cried for Jesse. And I cried for me.

Chapter
Twenty-nine

"From the beginning, it seemed clear to me that Jesse Southland was the person with the strongest motive for committing this murder," said Teresa.

We were in her office again. Bobby O'Hanlon was smiling at us from his corner of the desk. He seemed to be getting a kick out of this informal postmortem we were having. I had the feeling Teresa always shared them with him.

"But of course Jesse Southland was dead. Or so you all thought."

"Stupid us," I said.

"Not at all. Jesse was very clever. She set the stage. For months you'd been hearing through the property master that Ms. Southland was depressed and desperate. By the time the 'accident' occurred, you were primed. Psychologically, you'd been expecting something to happen. In a way, you might have been relieved: at least she hadn't died by her own hand."

"Jesse always said you could make the audience swallow anything if you set them up right." I didn't mean to sound bitter, the words just seemed to be coming out that way. Teresa, on the other hand, seemed to be having a swell time.

"And she set up all of it brilliantly," said Teresa. "The property master was the perfect choice to receive the news of Ms. Southland's 'death.' He's not an analytical man. And he'd be too upset to ask questions about the accident, or to recognize Ms. Southland's voice when she called as the general manager of the theater to give him the news."

"None of us could have recognized Jesse if she was doing a different voice. She was terrific with voices."

And if her routine almost killed poor little Tommy Props, what the hell? The show must go on.

"Leaving the money for her own party was a nice touch, but that was where she slipped up," Teresa continued. I looked at her in amazement; she really loved rehashing all this stuff. "Everything about her so-called death—the time of the accident, the place—was so vague, it would have been difficult to trace." Teresa got up and started pacing in her enthusiasm. It really was incredible the way she never bumped into that flag. "But when you told me the party was held two weeks after Ms. Southland's death, I knew we had something. It always takes longer than two weeks to probate a will."

"And that was the hunch which sent you to Ohio."

"I wanted to talk to the lawyer who sent that check. Ms. Southland had gone to him posing as her own friend, recently bereaved . . ."

"In black from head to toe, I bet. God, she was a one-woman acting company."

"She does seem to have used her talents most effectively. She gave the lawyer, a Mr. Alsrom, a story about her late friend who had left a sum of money which was to be sent on to your property master here in New York. Mr. Alsrom told me he remembered thinking at the time that the request was slightly unusual, but he chalked it up to the fact that Ms. Southland had been in show business."

Of course he did.

"Eventually her masquerade would have unraveled. If I'd had a few more days in Ohio . . ."

Teresa stopped and looked at me. For the first time she seemed to notice that I wasn't getting the same thrill out of this session that she was.

"I don't think Jesse realized how much pain she caused all of you, Angie," she said gently. "I think her need for revenge was just too strong . . ."

I nodded.

"She must have been a wonderful actress."

"Jesse was the best," I said.

Chapter Thirty

For almost two weeks we were big news. Then a megastar out in L.A. was slapped with a twenty-million-dollar palimony suit—I believe the custody of a pet llama was also at stake—and everyone forgot about us. Life got back to normal.

Except for the fact that Larry seemed to be avoiding me. Then one day he walked into my office.

"Hi, Ange," he said.

It didn't take a huge intellect to know what was up. Mostly because he was so happy.

"Congratulations," I said. "When did Chrissie come home?"

I waited for him to stiffen the way he always does when I get the jump on him. But he just smiled.

"Two nights ago. Congratulations to you, too."

"For?"

"A narrow escape. We came close to making the mistake of our lives."

"Speak for yourself."

"I'm not the man for you, Ange."

"I see. Well, thank you for sharing. And do close the door on your way out."

He walked over to my chair and sat down in it.

"You've always been so impressed by Larry the Wasp Prince. So I've never been able to tell you what it was like to grow up in a dynasty.

"Two or three minutes after they name you for one of the clan's overachievers, they let you know that there is a family tradition of excellence which you are expected to uphold. If it kills you. At about the time that other kids are getting applause for eating with their fingers, you're getting lectures on setting life goals. When the rest of your peer group is watching cartoons on television, you and your siblings are having algebra tournaments and playing word games designed to increase the vocabulary. Eventually you either become a credit to your ancestors or a drunk. The family tree is loaded with both. What we don't have are mediocrities. I'm probably the first."

"You're not mediocre. You're a damn good writer."

"No. What I do is 'cater to the lowest common denominator of vulgar taste.' At least, I think that's the way my father phrased it. I'm not whining. I know my childhood was not the stuff of *Oliver Twist*. But I hated it. And I learned to know what I didn't want for myself when I grew up."

"That would be me."

"I love you, Ange. I think I'll always love you. But I don't want to live with you. I want my home to be an easy place. I don't want a wife who's constantly challenging herself and me. I don't want her to be driven and ambitious. And stronger than I am. I do want her to need me very much. Your jaw is dropping, you'd better close your mouth."

I closed it.

Larry went on. "It gets worse. I want a wife who doesn't want to work outside the home. One of the privileges of my position is that I'll never need two incomes. I want my wife to take care of me, and our home, and our kids when we have them. But most of all, I want her to make me feel that I'm the center of her world."

"You're kidding."

"That makes me very happy, Ange. I don't even need it to be true. I just need her to make me feel it. And I'm not apologizing for that. Not anymore. I don't care how politically incorrect I am. The nineties be damned."

"And what happens if one day Chrissie decides she wants a life of her own?"

He smiled tenderly.

"Chrissie would find a way to do it without bruising my fragile ego."

There didn't seem to be anything else for me to say. Larry came over and kissed me on the top of the head. He started for the door, then turned.

"You're going to be okay, Ange. Better than okay. You've exorcised Jesse's ghost. And I'm not the man you thought I was. Now you can move on. Who knows? Someday you may even decide to leave *Bright Tomorrow*."

And he walked out.

As it turned out, I didn't decide to leave *Bright Tomorrow*. The decision was made for me. When I refused to bring Claire Wingate back on the show, Lucy Stone, the new Vice President in charge of Daytime at ABN, released me to pursue new and more exciting career opportunities.

At first I waited for the dream about Mama and the bathtub to start up again. When it didn't, I realized that I was going to be okay—better than okay.

I felt the way I do right before we tape a new show. The slate is clean and we're counting down. We're excited and a little nervous. We haven't made any mistakes yet, and there's the possibility that this time we're really going to nail it. It's all ahead of us. Anything can happen.